RARITAN PUBLIC LIBRARY
54 E. SOMERSET STREET
RARITAN, NEW JERSEY 08869
908-725-0413

9/18

KNIGHTS OF THE FORES†

by

ROBERT N. D'AMBOLA

First published by Dog Ear Publishing
4011 Vincennes Road
Indianapolis, IN 46268
www.dogearpublishing.net

ISBN: 978-1-4575-6250-1

This book is printed on acid free paper.
Printed in the United States of America

DEDICATION

This book is dedicated to my fellow Knights, who gave me the best childhood a kid could possibly ask for, to the outliers who made life interesting, and to all the pink ribbons who made the Bowl more fun, especially to my own pink ribbon who has made my life worth living.

To Michael, who left us too soon.

DISCLAIMER

I knew I was in trouble when I found out I had to include a disclaimer to this book. It's not like you are going to go out and hurt yourself with it. If you happen to manage that, you are on your own and you're not getting a dime from me for hurting yourself with a book. I believe I am on solid legal ground with that one.

First off, let me explain that this is a work of fiction. Yes, it is true that some of the events really happened, but there is enough BS filler to disqualify this story as non-fiction, or in that case, disqualify it as a work of art. Who knows, maybe in a few centuries public opinion will change. Many of the great masters died penniless and unknown. I'm definitely headed down the right path to achieve a place among them.

OK, now to the disclaiming part. In researching this story, (yes it's hard to believe I actually took the time and looked crap up), I discovered that there was another, actual group called Knights of the Forest. They were not as fun a group, as you will find out, as mine was. The originals were also not nice people.

The original Knights of the Forest were a very secret organization that was formed around the start of the Civil War. They were an evil lot, whose sole purpose was to rid Minnesota of Indians. This was a horrible time in American history when settlers wanted Indians removed from the area or totally exterminated because they were

Indians. The KOTF were responsible, either directly or indirectly, for the deaths of hundreds of members of the Sioux and Winnebago tribes.

I want to assure my readers that I abhor all of the treatment towards America's first residents and do not wish to glorify the original KOTF in any manner. There is little written about the original KOTF group, as it was a well kept secret and members pledged not to reveal any information to others. Please know that no Native Americans were harmed in the writing of this book.

Note: If you don't read the Forward you will lose the point of the story and may as well throw the book away or use it to prop up that crooked table you never got around to fixing. Just do not hurt yourself with this book. You have been warned.

TABLE OF CONTENTS

FOREWORD

There have been many famous forests mentioned throughout time, history and literature, but I'm guessing you probably weren't paying attention so here is my summary. When I was a young boy, I was tricked into learning about several forests without giving my consent. The first ones that come to mind are of course your standard Enchanted Forests. This is always a place involving magic and strange creatures that usually want to eat you. Sometimes the poor victims that reside within these forests were changed into some sad creature, because they pissed off an ugly old witch. They should have known to avoid these witches in the first place, so they get no pity from me. The definition of enchanted forest states: it is a place containing enchantment. Who saw that one coming?

My kindly, old, third grade teacher always read us stories about Christopher Robin's Hundred Acre Wood, based on the real-life *Five Hundred Acre Wood* in Ashdown Forest, located in East Sussex, England. Had Winnie-the-Pooh, (WTP to his close friends), been a vicious, Piglet eating bear, the Hundred Acre Wood would have also classified as an Enchanted Forest, and also would have created a generation of deeply disturbed children with serious bacon issues.

When I was a bit older, children were required to watch *The Wizard of Oz* on Thanksgiving, so parents could get some peace during the holiday. In this movie

Dorothy traveled through the Haunted Forest on her cross-country, LSD trip, to Oz. If she had murdered one more witch, she would have been considered a serial killer and the movie would have had a different twist. Serial killers are required to kill at least three people to qualify for this status – not my rule. Less than three kills, places you in the extremely bad person category. The name, Haunted Forest, was really misleading because there was no haunting anywhere to be found. This forest was inhabited by a group of not so intelligent apple trees with bad attitudes and worse aim.

One of my favorite movies was *The Princess Bride*. There was an interesting forest in this story that was referred to as The Fire Swamp, so it may not technically be classified as a forest. This desirable vacation spot had a mixture of the Fire Spurt, Lightning Sand, and of course the R.O.U.S., (Rodents of Unusual Size), which I do not think exist. I believe that these elements qualify the Fire Swamp as an Enchanted Forest, but who am I to judge?

And of course there is my all-time favorite; Sherwood Forest, where swashbuckling, Robin Hood and his Merry Men, (not that there is anything wrong with that), hung out and harassed the government. It is a shame swashbuckler is no longer a career choice. I mistakenly believed Sherwood to be a mythical place, but it really does exist in, go figure, Nottingham, England.

I will tell you about the evils of school later, but one of the things they pushed on us was geography. This was a concept that was beyond my grasp. One place that I did remember was also the best-named forest, The Black Forest or Schwarzwald, located in southwestern Germany. I do not know if it is indeed a black forest or someone named it that because they thought it sounded cool. It is definitely a cool name. I have never been there but I have eaten the cake made famous by this location. I still do not get the connection. I am told that there is also a Black Forest ham, however I have no idea what that is all about. Maybe Piglet relocated, to get away from that annoying Christopher, to achieve better Feng Shui.

Two forests that I had personal experience with were the Amazon Rain Forest and the Redwood Forest. The Amazon Rain Forest is the only forest I know of that has it's own restaurant franchise. I have patronized at least two of their locations and found the burgers to be excellent. The Amazon Rain Forest is the granddaddy of all forests. It is slightly smaller than an Amazon distribution center, hence its name. It is as large as the continental United States and covers nine countries in South America. Please don't ask me to name them because as I have stated, I am horrible at geography and can't name the fifty states. I have trouble keeping track of right and left. People are currently trying their best to see how fast they can reduce this breathtaking forest area to the size of a Christmas tree lot on December 26th, because humans are stupid and don't see the big picture. We have plenty of air so why don't we cut down millions of trees and destroy the planet?

You would think that the largest forest would have the largest trees. This is not the case, as God plays by his own rules. The largest trees are found in the Redwood Forest in California. I had a chance to go there as a child and seeing the giant Sequoias up close really gives you a perspective of where people rate up against nature. If it were up to Mother Nature, we wouldn't rate at all. She would do just fine without us; actually much better. (See: Amazon Rain Forest)

In my feeble attempt to provide an educational boost to this story, I looked up the definition of a forest. Apparently there is no one real definition of a forest as there are over 800 definitions of a forest around the world. I will attempt to wrap this discussion up by providing this example. In their landmark case on defining pornography, the United States Supreme Court ruled that, you would know it when you see it. I guess forests fall into the same category as pornography. This is my last attempt at providing knowledge.

For the sake of brevity, I shall use my own personal definition of a forest, which is a place where there is any amount of trees that would be sufficient to make you happy enough to call it a forest. I had my own forest growing up as a child. It wasn't enchanted or haunted. It wasn't grand or significant enough to attract tourists. There were no historic battles fought there to my knowledge. It wasn't a color or an adjective. As a matter of fact, it didn't even have a name. I didn't own the forest but was fortunate enough to borrow it for a few years, along with a bunch of great friends. We became the Knights of the Forest and this is our story.

CHAPTER ONE

MEIN WAY OR THE HIGHWAY

Over 15 million members of the military returned home to the United States after defeating the pure evil that caused WWII. This victory, along with the GI bill of 1944, that provided affordable mortgages for veterans, stimulated a boom in housing construction, which led to the growth of the wondrous land that would be soon known as, and forever referred to as, Suburbia. So in a sick, twisted way, Hitler not only was responsible for the deaths of over 50 million people world-wide, but also for my childhood, and the path that evolved from there. Hitler impacted the course of my life. Does this mean I have to send the sick, psychotic, Nazi-bastard a posthumous thank you note? Not gonna happen.

While bad-guy Hitler created the housing and baby boom, good-guy Eisenhower was responsible for building the United States Interstate Highway System. Ike had been impressed with the German roads while he was there during WWII, and he wanted them for his own country. Ok so we have to give psycho-stache some credit for this too. After Dwight became President, he had the Federal-Aid Highway Act of 1956, authorize $25 billion for the construction of a 41,000-mile "National System of Interstate Highways." The History Channel tells us that:

The new interstate highways were controlled-access expressways with no at-grade crossings–that is, they had overpasses and underpasses instead of intersections. They were at least four lanes wide and were designed for high-speed driving. They were intended to serve several purposes: eliminate traffic congestion; replace what one highway advocate called "undesirable slum areas" with pristine ribbons of concrete; make coast-to-coast transportation more efficient.

So let us recap the Fed Highway Plan:

- Yes, it created high-speed driving, now bordering on the insane.
- As far as eliminating traffic: these roads were also supposed to make it easy for people to survive an atomic attack! That's a cheery thought but no one expected the rapid growth of the "Rush Hour" that totally immobilized all traffic, for the required one-hour time period, to get to and from work, which eventually grew to three hours in the morning and three hours in the evening. And this was during peacetime when everyone wasn't fighting for <u>his</u> ultimate survival. (Sorry, women were not a big part of the workforce yet). Another small point that this added benefit of evacuation missed, was that it would have been unlikely that the government would have been nice enough to make an announcement that millions of Americans were about to be incinerated in a fiery ball of light, in the time it takes to turn on the ignition in your Rambler. All they had to do was watch what happens when a storm rolls into shore on a summer weekend when there is no order to be found, nor well-mannered families anywhere, heading to main arteries. They will do anything not to get caught in traffic. Chaos rules the road.

- Rumor also had it that these highways were designed and built so one in five miles are straight, to accommodate military aircraft for landing purposes. I'm not commenting either way on that one, because my brain hurts thinking about it.
- And there is nothing like miles of pristine concrete to spruce up the environment.

The Greatest Generation had defeated the Axis of Evil and couldn't wait to put on their spiffy drab green uniforms again. It only took a few years before we headed off to Korea. At least this time they shortened the fighting to three years although the TV show lasted eleven. This was an undeclared war because America didn't want to hurt anyone's feeling and it was way too soon for a big number III. The Korean Conflict ended on July 27, 1953, not with surrender, but with a truce, with both sides promising not to go in each other's yard, ever again. America was glad they never had to deal with North Korea again. The Knights would arrive the following year during almost peacetime.

CHAPTER TWO

THERE'S NO PLACE LIKE HOME

After the roads were built, developers were in housing heaven, as they gobbled up open spaces of farmland that were no longer worth the time and trouble to plow, compared to the windfall they would get for the sale of their vacant land. One "prime" selection of land lay adjacent to one of the original New Jersey highways, Rt. 22. This highway dissected the state, running west, from Newark at the Atlantic Ocean to Phillipsburg at the Pennsylvania border.

Engineers saw a vision of 200 single-family homes on 2500 square foot lots. They carved out the side of a large hill and inserted a half-mile oval at the bottom of the pit to insert the various tract homes around it, similar to a Monopoly board game. (Fortunately all the homes were not green and orange hotels were not in the design plan.) Their total-use development ambition of the site was stifled by the fact that the Elizabeth River ran through the edge of the property, cutting off approximately 50 acres, deemed as unbuildable due to flooding when the river became angry.

This was an important turning point, not quite as impactful as Hitler and WWII, but important nonetheless, so pay attention. You are allowed to take notes if you wish. This decision let stand a tree-filled buffer, running up to and continuing on the other side of the river and up another hillside. It would take almost a decade of evolution before small urchins would inhabit this remaining unnamed "forest".

While houses began springing out of, what was once rows of vegetables, the State of New Jersey was spending its share of federal highway money for its own massive transportation project. New Jersey was completing the 172-mile-long, limited-access tollroad, which became known as the Garden State Parkway. The tolls were only 10 cents per county but the good news was they promised that the tolls would be removed after the road was paid for. Like all moneymaking ventures, the government found it too lucrative to give up, once the coins started adding up faster than they could wrap them in their designated little paper folders. Decades later, the tolls collected over almost half a billion dollars per year. Vehicular volume rapidly increased into the hundreds of millions of happy motorists, driving upon pristine ribbons of concrete.

The Parkway would set the fourth boundary of this new development to the north, with Rt. 22 on the south, the 100 ft. hill to the east, and the Forest to the west. The perfect ingredients were now in place for life to spring forth again, as it had done millions of years ago on young planet Earth. This time when the simple life forms crawled out of the primordial swamp, they had Buicks.

Young married couples flocked to the "Parkway Estates" in droves and plunked down their newly acquired federal mortgage money for the privilege to own their very own $20,000, three-bedroom piece of the American Dream. This dream came complete with a single-car attached garage and their very own yard, dog not included. A home that, over the next few decades, would actually cost them ten times what they had agreed to pay for it. Most of the couples were already happily in the process of creating the first round of Baby Boomers (it is a proven fact that war makes you horny). Boomer was the demographic moniker of all people born between 1946 and 1964. The acquisition of a home only perpetuated the reproductive instinct so a second round of Boomers were put into production. The new parents would soon be required by the United States Census Bureau to have 2.5 children to meet U.S. standards. Most adults were not able to understand how to achieve the ½% child so they acquired a dog for the empty yard, which was deemed acceptable by the government, thus fulfilling the requirement.

This new population of Boomers arrived just in time for the Cold War that unofficially kicked off in 1947. Let's say it was very chilly at this time. Boomers were taught self-preservation by taking shelter under their wooden school desks in the event of an attack. Everyone was well aware that even though an entire city could be reduced to ashes in a matter of seconds, a wooden school desk would afford the appropriate shield to survive an atomic blast of over 10,000 degrees F, as was in the case in Hiroshima. As if atomic bombs were not scary enough, scientists worked harder and developed a hydrogen weapon capable of achieving a blast temperature of several million degrees within one millionth of a second. Under these circumstances, taking shelter under a wooden school desk would not be recommended.

CHAPTER THREE

GOOD FENCES MAKE GOOD NEIGHBORS

P oet Robert Frost must have had an interesting experience when he wrote *The Mending Wall*. Something happened in his life to make him come to the realization that a fence is a bold statement. It defines a perimeter as well as ownership and ensures privacy. One by one the single-family, split-level structures sprung up in what would be later referred to as The Bowl. Foundations were dug, creating basements as the footprints of the homes. Skeletal frames grew out of the dark gray cinderblock abyss. Specialized electrical crews were subcontracted to install the central nervous systems of each of these wooden creatures. The homes would have all indoor plumbing, something to which the "Greatest Generation" was not always accustomed, and most likely, not their parents. Most of us kids would now have our own bedroom. Our parents were lucky if they didn't have to share a bed with more than one person.

The inner circle of homes numbered about fifty with all the rears facing inward. This was a "circle the wagons" type configuration. It was actually a large half-mile oval. This left a great common area running over 1,000 feet in length between the homes at the farthest ends. It's too bad that landscape designers and community planners did not exist at this time. This area could have served as the heart of the development with a shared purpose for socializing and gatherings. The great space could have been created with a meandering path to stroll or to walk Fido. There could have been park benches, a gazebo, and a flagpole to show patriotism. A fountain or two would have completed the Zen-like atmosphere. This was not to be.

Instead, new homeowners immediately staked out their property and began installing fences around their respective lots. One main reason for a fence to be erected was that these modern house designs moved the outdoor family recreation area from the once grand front porches of older model homes, to the rear, what became known as patios. Patios were usually square slabs of bland cement that eventually were used to park a wooden picnic table on. This was an essential component for barbeques and kid birthday parties because you can hose everything down after the candles are blown out and not mess up the interior. The trick is to have a summer baby. I was lucky enough to be a summer baby. Timing is everything.

All the family celebrations and relaxation time were then in full view of the common area of the development. This was unacceptable. People had moved out to the suburbs to get away from anthill living of urban cities. They wanted something cities didn't afford to residents, privacy. Suburbanites found that peeing on the perimeter to mark their territory did not deter trespassers. A few tried to maintain that country aspect with a split rail fence. This invoked images of living at the corral. The majority of homeowners installed the basic, four-foot, silver, metal, chain-link fence, which clearly said don't come in my yard. This also diminished the neighborly atmosphere. The brave-hearted tried to surround their property with hedges. Shrubbery does not stop anything from passing through either way. Once the family decided that they needed a puppy, a secondary barrier went up to supplement the greenery, usually a four-foot high, silver, metal, chain-link fence, to keep Fido contained. The great open expanse that existed, ever so briefly, in the center of the oval, was divvied up like an apple pie on Thanksgiving, and then modified into mini fortresses. This eliminated the common space as a play area for the hordes of crumb-crunchers to come. The great space would have served this purpose well, as stay-at-home moms could have been able to lovingly glance out their kitchen windows to see what their little muffins were up to. This was still a time when children went OUT to play, so this was yet another monumental decision that forced the children to go somewhere else for entertainment. All the pieces of the puzzle were now in place.

Marilyn Monroe married Joe DiMaggio in 1954. McCarthy started his communist shenanigans finding enemies everywhere. Vice President Richard Nixon announced that the U.S. was sending our boys to Indochina (probably another temporary matter). It had been a secret that the United States had started getting involved in Vietnam as early as 1950. It should have been called Vietnam Part II because France had already failed there.

The words "Under God" were added to the Pledge of Allegiance because there was a need to find God again, with all those Communists running about. Ellis Island was closed while the first Burger King opened. There has to be some type of irony there somewhere.

CHAPTER FOUR

FIRST ROUND

W hen the families started to populate their new homesteads, some brought the first round of young-uns in tow. The oldest child in the entire neighborhood was probably no more than six years old upon arrival. The parents willingly pulled them out of whatever school they had been attending because the suburbs offered a promise of a new life, if the children wanted it or not. These kids would get over it, with probably little or no therapy.

First-Rounders were all very content in their own little world. They were the princes and princesses of the castle. They were the first born and received 100% of the attention from both parents along with visiting relatives and friends. They received all the gifts for every occasion. They were the center of the universe. It would be a traumatic day for First-Rounders when they found out that Copernicus discovered the earth revolves around the sun and not them. They hated Copernicus. They had mom and dad tightly wound around their precious little finger. Any whimper would result in a mad dash to make sure that junior was not choking on his or her silver spoon.

First-Rounders had it, as they used to say, made in the shade. Life was good, that is, until their evil nemesis arrived. The first thought they had upon learning of a new arrival was, "how do I get rid of it." The saying goes, *"Siblings - you can't live with'em and you can't kill'em."* That didn't mean the First-Rounders didn't try.

The next best thing to elimination was sabotage. First-Rounders would learn us bad. I remember my own sister teaching me to count: one, two, three, chicken, five. For the longest time I thought the color blue was called fork. They also fed us whatever they could when there was limited adult supervision. I developed an uncanny taste for Milk Bones - they aren't really that bad. To this day I salivate every time I hear the command to sit.

Before Second-Rounders could talk, First-Rounders could dole out physical punishment as they pleased, without the chance of the younger sibling ratting them out. A slight smack would be enough to make the toddler cry. When the parental unit responded the FR would get away with an excuse as simple as, "he stuck his bummy in the electrical outlet." What does that mean? I do not believe this action is even a possibility. The parent would buy into this lame excuse 100% because precious No. 1 could never do anything wrong.

Another favorite scheme was to spin the child around until they puked. This worked best after a hearty meal. Success was guaranteed if the perpetrator fled the scene before the eruption for total deniability. First-Rounders were an evil lot that preyed on the weak as long as they could get away with it.

CHAPTER FIVE

SECOND ROUND

W e are not going to concern ourselves with the First-Rounders because this is not about them. There were hundreds of photographs taken and miles of bad black & white, 8mm film documenting everything they did. "Look Mary, little Frank is drooling, get a picture." By the time the second round showed up, parents were exhausted. There would be a drastic drop off in the amount of recording of crucial events. No notations were made on the back of the photos with the curly edges, so any future references were merely guesses. I think that is Johnny dressed as a clown? What was he, seven?

I said I was lucky to be a summer baby but that's where the luck stopped. We members of the second round had to share everything. The Second-Rounders arrived anywhere from two to four years after the first round. My theory on this is it takes that long to forget how much work the first round really was. I call it baby amnesia. Humans have short memories and will often repeat their mistakes if enough time elapses. Prime example – World War II, no lessons learned from World War I. At first they will curse the sleepless nights, the constant diaper changes, the endless cleaning, and never eating a hot meal, until they catch baby amnesia and say, "I think we need a little (Insert one – brother or sister)."

This is the ONLY thing that the First-Rounders did not get to vote on.

Black Americans were getting more frustrated at their second-class status and being treated unfairly, sometimes with violence. There was a growing civil rights movement. Meanwhile, in 1953, the white folks were having their own movement, getting frisky after watching movies like *From Here to Eternity, Gentlemen Prefer Blondes,* and *Roman Holiday.* This created the unintentional consequences of the second round of boomers born in the Bowl. The consequences would be 20 pink and blue ribbons hung out on the doors the following year.

Now I love babies as much as the next fellow, especially when I was one of the new crowd, but human babies are pretty much the most useless creature, that God has ever whipped up. They can't do anything for a really long time after birth and can really kill a party. They also smell awful. For goodness sake, baby sea turtles have more going for them right out of the egg than a human being. Of course there is a great chance the baby turtle will be eaten by a sea gull before they complete that first crawl back to the ocean. Life is not perfect.

Scientific American estimated a human fetus would have to undergo a gestation period of 18 to 21 months, instead of the usual nine, to be born at a neurological and cognitive development stage comparable to that of a chimpanzee newborn.

Another by-product of WWII was the CDC (Center for Disease Control & Prevention). This is another over-sized government organization that figured out something after years of excruciating research and the expenditure of millions of dollars. That would be the Infant Developmental Milestones:

- First two months – babies can't lift their heads
- 4 months – roll over

- 6 months – sit up
- 9 months – start standing
- 1 year – start walking

Of course we have known this for thousands of years and I believe it was Moses that said, after observing his one year old firstborn son, Gersom, "According to the IDM, shouldn't he be parting a sea by now?"

Let me shed some light on this scientific statement. A longer gestation period would not serve anyone well, trust me. Males would undergo unbelievably harsh conditions if pregnancies were doubled. Sure it would be cool to have a chimp baby but not at this price. The stretch mark argument alone is not worth the effort.

The useless years for the Second-Rounders were very historic, although we had no idea there was a world beyond our binky:

In 1955 Rosa Parks decided she wasn't going to sit in the back of the bus anymore, officially setting off the Civil Rights Movement. What she did not know was that a person sitting in the front of the bus was more likely to sustain serious injuries from a head-on collision.

In 1956 Elvis Presley hit the charts with Heartbreak Hotel, Don Larsen threw the only perfect game in a World Series, and almost serial killer Dorothy made it to television. The Wizard of Oz became a yearly tradition.

In 1957, something called a space race started. How do you race in space when there is no up, down, or gravity? America would soon find out, and we were already losing it.

THE FIRST STAGE OF KNIGHTHOOD

S ure you thought I forgot what this book was about. Your saying to yourself right now, "For Pete's sake, and I don't know who Pete is, it's chapter six already. Where the heck are the Knights?" Sorry it's called plot development and I tend to ramble so untighten the wad in your panties and sit back. We're getting there. Refer to your copious notes if you're having a problem following this story. It's not rocket science.

I first met some of the Knights after some of my initial cognitive skills had developed. See how I fit that in. There was no such thing as play dates back in the fifties. Parents didn't put babies together to slobber on each other so they could interact with real humans. They, and I mean the moms, endured their sentence of isolation with their babbling shit tornados by themselves.

The moms' one outlet was to go for a walk. Baby carriages were about the size and weight of a Cadillac of the era complete with tail fins. The wheels were the size of tractor tires. They were connected to a truck suspension system that could bounce a full-grown adult across the street. The body of the carriage was a massive structure encased by a heavy fabric similar to bulletproof Kevlar, covered by a retractable hood. The frame was of industrial steel. Plastic had not come into fashion, because no one had watched The Graduate yet, to pick up on that tidbit of information. The entire unit probably weighed about a buck fifty. The only portable aspect of these baby yachts was that some models collapsed down to the suspension making it lower but just as hard to pick up. This really did not classify as portable.

Moms would somehow maneuver this contraption out to the sidewalk, probably leaving the baby unattended in the house, and then retrieve junior for "The Walk." The child could not see anything but sky, if they were even awake, but the air was good for them. Pollution had not yet been invented. At least it gave the moms a chance to light up their favorite cigarettes during their healthy walk.

There are five official stages of Knighthood: Background, Upbringing, Page, Squire, and Knight. The first two stages were predetermined by our respective sets of parents. Our folks had made the decision to move to this neighborhood carved out of a hillside. They were respectable people and instilled in us their values, patriotism, and overall goodness. In other words, they tried their best not to raise a bunch of assholes.

The first unofficial rendezvous for the Knights would be Kindergarten. We would have had to attain the age of five years old to make the cut to get into class. This would make us Pages until the age of seven. We were totally unaware of our predetermined destiny and the path that we would eventually follow to Knighthood.

We met on the giant red circle, painted on the old faded wooden floor in the center of the room. This was the first divine sign that the Knights would be formed to emulate the courage of the legendary round table of King Arthur. The King had selected this shape to represent equal status among all that sat around his table. There would be no head position.

We may have only been five years old, but there was no mistaking who was in charge of the room. The true boss was the lumberjack size lady wearing the flowery dress that looked like my grandmother's bedspread. Her giant clunky shoes added to her height, not that she needed it. She was already bigger than most of our fathers. You would usually know when she was near you before you saw her because she smelled like a flower garden that had gone bad in the sun.

Our teacher was friendly and approachable, despite her intimidating appearance. She beat the yellow, Have A Nice Day smiley face, to the punch by a decade. Unfortunately for her, she did not copyright the phrase and was doomed to an existence on a teacher's salary. There was no doubt who ran the circle.

To be perfectly honest, at this point of our lives, we didn't know the circle was there because we weren't smart enough to know shapes. We did not have Sesame Street to teach us all that good shit upon exiting the womb. There were no pre-school programs to prepare you for the trauma of kindergarten. We also had no idea what a desk was for. The school figured it was a safe bet was that we couldn't fall off of the floor, although some of us tried hard.

It always amazed me that parents would go through the trouble of teaching their babies an incorrect baby-talk language to purposely create stupid toddlers. Why don't they teach them the correct words the first time so they don't have to take an English as a Second Language course? Parents may have understood that knowledge is power and they didn't want to give that up quite yet.

The group would not be completed for some time for various reasons. One reason was that Kindergarten was only a half day. Some of us went to morning class while the rest attended the afternoon session. I was lucky enough to get the morning gig. I'm still a morning person but I can no longer sit Indian style, which by the way, is now politically incorrect.

Mornings were best because everything was fresh and clean from the janitor's efforts from the previous night's work. The room did not smell of bodily fluids, including puke. Kindergarten was very stressful for some. The toys were all in place and the teacher had not yet reached critical meltdown for the day, as they had to do every day's activities twice! I don't know how one person controlled a room full of whirling dervishes without wrapping them up in their binky blankets and stuffing their little bodies in their respective cubby spaces.

A.M. class got to go home for lunch and stay there for extended afternoon play. You didn't have to stay clean all day, which is impossible for a 5-year-old, and the best thing of all was you got to take an afternoon nap. Adults forget that this is the best thing in the world. Naps are like crack for kids. Even though you may not know where you are when you wake up, it's free. Naps should be written into all business contracts. The world would be a better place with a well-rested population.

Another reason the Knights were splintered was that there was a shitload of Second-Rounders. Too many, in fact, to fit into one class, so our group ran two classes all the way through grammar school. We didn't start to fully socialize until big boy, full day first grade. We were men then with little or no crap in our pants. Our mothers, on the other hand, thought we were living during the Renaissance and dressed us, let's say, *fancy*, until our testicles fully dropped and we knew enough to complain about it. I hold the theory that most boys are somewhat gay until they are seven years old. After my fashion rebellion, my mother thought I was Johnny Cash because I would only wear black. *I didn't wear black for the poor and the beaten down, livin' in the hopeless, hungry side of town.* *I didn't wear it for the prisoner, who has long paid for his crime, but there because he's a victim of the times.* I wore black for no apparent reason and I had never heard of Johnny Cash.

On Jan 7,1959, the US recognized the new Cuban Government of Fidel Castro. He was an affable urban guerrilla, freedom fighter, with a serious fashion statement, who no one believed would stay in power for more than a few years. The next month America successfully test-fired a Titan intercontinental ballistic missile lovingly referred to as an ICBM. I have no idea what this would have to do with Castro.

The first seven "Mercury" astronauts were named to compete in that space race thing. Alaska became our 49th state and finally completed our national flag with another star.

CHAPTER SEVEN

THE CASTLE

I believe the true inspiration for The Knights was the fact that we spent our days within the confines of the castle. The castle was our grammar school. It is unclear when this structure was built, as there is no cornerstone to commemorate the occasion. I can only surmise that it was in a time when architects had freedom to design a structure, free from boring cookie cutter plans and meddling Boards of Education, because this building was awesome. It resembled 12th century, Sterling Castle, in Scotland, from a once-noble era.

The building was constructed entirely of faded red brick and had giant twin turrets rising on both sides of the massive wooden front door. You expected the door to be lowered by immense clanging chains instead of swinging open. The sidewalls extended back in a 45-degree angle from the front entrance, giving the illusion of greater height, due to position of the turrets. There were only two floors to the building but it appeared more massive as it sat on a slightly higher elevation than the surrounding property, similar to its sister across the ocean. This, however, was somewhat of an optical illusion. The fact that we were only three feet tall may also have had something to do with our perception of the size of the building. The castle at Disney World is also built with a similar illusion. That little bastard rodent has been deceiving us all this time.

The rear of the building was divided into two triangle shaped courtyards. This area would be our assembly points prior to entering school. They kept boys on one court and the girls on the other for some inexplicable reason, possibly to prevent breeding. We hadn't yet read the masturbation handbook but they thought we would impregnate someone. An aerial view of the building would show it to look something similar to the modern fixed wing Stealth Bomber.

Our castle was called Calvin Coolidge, after one of the most boring Presidents in history, the 30th to be exact. Old Silent Cal was noted for leading our nation into the Great Depression. It was too early to name the school after JFK, as it would be several decades after the school was constructed before Kennedy took his infamous convertible drive through Dallas.

There were very few exterior doors, as building codes were more lax. This made defending the castle easier, so maybe they were onto something back then. There was no such thing as school shootings such as the horrific Texas tower incident. That first mass school shooting wouldn't take place for a few more years. The only thing missing from our castle was a moat. I would spend close to 9,000 hours of my childhood as a prisoner of the castle. The good news was they didn't make me wear the iron mask during my confinement. I believe the Curse of Calvin's Depression was alive and well in old CC.

We understood it wasn't a real castle; however, it had its own torture chamber. The adults called it the playground. The well-meaning and clueless school board reasoned that us little tykes needed an area to burn up excessive energy so we would be more receptive to learning when we came back inside. They reached out to a well-known company familiar with this mission. I believe it was called Satan's Playgrounds. They constructed contraptions for our amusement that would rival those used during the Inquisition. Adults made the fatal mistake of believing that their children would operate the equipment as it was intended. When did that ever happen?

First of all, every piece of equipment was constructed of heavy gauge steel probably left over from WWII scrap ship metal. This required enormous matching bolts to connect it all together. These bolts would protrude perilously from all points, where the metal was joined, creating flesh-catching, clothes-ripping hazards. You were guaranteed to "find" these bolts every time you ran around an obstacle or grabbed the top of one. The special attribute of these bolts was that they rusted immediately upon installation. Serious infection and a condition called lockjaw could result from introduction of dirt and rust into an open wound. The bolts were very successful in opening wounds, however, we never witnessed anyone experiencing total body muscle spasms. That would have been so cool.

The swings looked innocent enough while they stood motionless but so does a rattlesnake. Unfortunately, the entire purpose of swings was for them to move. They became pendulums of death in our little hands. The seats were two-inch thick, unprotected hardwood boards. Any contact with your head would knock you into next Thursday. These seats were supported by two battleship anchor chains with links large enough to snap your fingers, again attached by killer bolts, at the top of the cross beam. We discovered one unintended use of the swing. That was to twist it as you sat on it. This would tighten the chains to a critical torque rotation and simultaneously lift the seat higher. You were almost guaranteed to catch some part of your body in the twisted chain.

The seats would eventually weather and create splinters large enough to harpoon Moby Dick, or in this case a small child. Everyone, meaning us kids, understood that the ultimate goal of the swing was to go high enough to circle the bar in one motion. This was another impossible dream of instant death that was fortunately never achieved. Many adventurous lads tried this feat while standing up on the seat. They would reach a height that would place their feet over their heads. The severely stupid would jump off at the apex of trajectory. This would send them sailing through the air only to crumple into the ground in a hard landing. We never thought that motion out to the end.

The merry-go-round was anything but merry. It depended solely on kid power to achieve maximum rotation momentum. Everyone would start out grabbing onto a critically installed metal bar and start running counter clockwise. I never understood if this direction was required or if running clockwise would unscrew the mechanism from the foundation, thus sending it sailing into the air. This was contrary to the righty tighty, lefty loosey rule.

One by one the munchkin power sources would jump onto the platform and hang on for dear life, as centrifugal force would attempt to fling them off. The last guy to hop on was lucky if he was not dragged underneath the swirling disk. The object of this ride was of course to make you puke. What else would a spinning object be used for? If you felt the feeling coming on and asked your friends to stop the ride, they would oblige you by going faster. What are friends for?

The slide had more hazards than adults could possibly dream of. The ladder climbed approximately twelve feet high, constructed, of course, with metal rungs. When wet, these rungs became extremely slippery for little scurrying feet. When, not if, you slipped off the step, you would either bang your shins against the lower rung or face plant into the upper rung. Either contact would be extremely painful.

The slide itself was another matter. The surface would often reach baking temperatures hot enough to cook small child buns, especially the back of your unprotected legs. The heat would prevent you from holding on so you rode down hands free and out of control. Sometimes the heat was so bad that it removed all friction from the surface and caused your body to be halted midway down the incline. The slide had an evil mind of its own. It captured its prey in a hold similar to a Venus flytrap and cooked its meal on the spot. No matter how hot the weather was there was always a muddy puddle at the bottom of the slide. If you didn't execute a two point landing correctly at the bottom, then you wound up with your butt in the puddle.

Of course we had to exponentially increase the risk factor by running up the slide, usually while someone was coming down. Again, this created endless possibilities for injuries. You could face plant on the slide if the surface was fast enough on that particular day, shoot directly off the slide and land mangled on the ground, or get your legs taken out by the rider, thus injuring both of you in one motion.

The pinnacle of insane equipment was the seesaw. This device is based upon the fulcrum theory to lift objects. It consisted of a long, narrow, hard wooden board (with eventual splinters), supported by a (soon-to-be, rusted) metal bar, located at the midpoint of the board. The ideal objective of this instrument was to go up and down. This is a simple concept: however the perfect operation of the seesaw depended upon two crucial elements. The first element was to have equal weight distribution at both end points of the board to allow the even up and down movement. The second critical factor was the presence of mutual trust among the participants.

Neither of these requirements ever existed together and it was near possible to achieve this combination in the first place. Adults set the playground bar extremely high on this play item. In the best-case scenario, you would have a set of identical twins on either side of the seesaw and even that would not guarantee a successful mission. One would always get the other at peak height of the board and then drop off the back allowing the stranded party to plummet to their death. Well maybe not death, but at least to a very hard ass-jarring landing, felt up into their teeth. There were no amount of swears, pinky or on a dead relative, that would prevent one of the participants to double cross the other and airdrop them. Both parties knew they had to do it to the other one first, before it happened to them. There was nothing better than playground equipment to build childhood distrust and cynicism.

My favorite piece was the jungle gym. This was a contortion of numerous, what else but, metal pipes. It looked as if an angry bunch of disturbed plumbers had a disagreement over how to hook up the bathroom sink. We would climb, swing, and hang off these pipes in any haphazard manner. Adults either did not have knowledge or any belief in gravity, or thought their little pumpkins were immune from these forces. We were not. The only thing missing from the already slippery bars was petroleum jelly to hasten your release.

The best part of the "playground" was the ground. They built these Darwin challenges on asphalt, or as we called it, the black top. Maybe the adult mindset was that we wouldn't get dirty or ruins our nice school clothes (not to be confused with play clothes). They never anticipated us landing on this surface in every unacceptable manner. We set out to disprove adult safety theories and succeeded in many horrifying ways. Many of us still bear the scars from our hard fought battles against playground equipment.

In 1961 a young whippersnapper was inaugurated as the 35th President of the United States. Although JFK would only serve a little more than 1,000 days in office, he was to leave a lasting imprint on America, the world, and beyond. He immediately saw the quick heat up to the Cold War when the Berlin Wall was constructed and he finally decided it wouldn't be that difficult to take out that pesky, cigar smoking guerrilla fighter in Cuba. That other problem in far-off Vietnam now included 2,000 of our boys. We were told that they were fighting over something called The Domino Principle. I never saw any worth to a bunch of black tiles with tiny white spots. We all assumed this matter should be resolved quickly with that many people involved.

CHAPTER EIGHT

THE KNIGHTS

This was a time that every child walked to and from school, which included lunchtime. The school administrators meticulously plotted designated walking routes to school for our safety. A school crossing guard covered each intersection. This was an eighth grader that was far superior to us younger children. They knew better than us and had the power of the white safety belt across their chest to prove their authority, plus they could, would, and did, beat us up. A paid guard, usually a retiree or mom, with time to handle a three-time a day post, manned the busy intersections. In the 60s, everyone walked to school unless it was extremely bad weather and then that wasn't a guarantee. The distance was under a mile but it would take our group almost a half an hour to make the trek because we were kids. Kids do not walk like normal people as it was against our nature. We did not follow straight lines. We could have made the distance in a fraction of the time when we were running late. Our parents always bragged to us that they walked miles to school, in a blizzard, uphill – both ways with no shoes. We didn't care.

I lived in the middle of the oval on the opposite side of the hill so I was the first in the walking chain. They call it a walking bus today but no kids walk to school now, even if they live across the street from the school building. I had to leave my house 10 minutes earlier to gather the rest of the future Knights. Sometimes Anthony Martini (The Mechanic) would walk down the hill and meet me. We would then head to Harry Kanakis' (Knapsack) house, across the street from me, but down a bit. His house sat at the edge of the Forest. As we followed the oval in a counter-clockwise direction, we would pick up Tommy Carroll (Tommy Gun or Gun for short), Frank Canko (Hoops), Joe Feeney (Skip), William Bodenhagen (Billy the Kid, The Kid or just Bo), and round off the group with Steve Cohen (Stevarino, which we adjusted to Rhino).

It was tough for anyone to come up with a nickname for me that would stick. I was always Robert to my family, never Bob or even Rob. I guess we were very formal. When I got older I was called Bob at work to distinguish me from the other Roberts that had arrived first. A few close people called me Bobby D. I think my favorite moniker was Bobert, but the gang just called me D.

If you took the bunch of us and stood us against a wall according to size, we would resemble a dysfunctional xylophone. Bo would be the highest note followed in sequence by: Rhino, Knapsack, Mechanic, me, Skip, Gun, and of course, Hoops as the lowest note, being the tallest. Height was the first characteristic we had available to us to compare ourselves with our peers. We would often stand back to back to hear the official verdict of the designated measurerer as to who was the tallest. We would do this even with the unlikely match-ups, such as Hoops vs. Bo. Hoops had like a foot on Bo but they needed to undergo this ritual to make it official. It's a kid thing.

Heights would change drastically as the years passed. Each guy would reach his growth spurt at a different age.

Bo always remained last and never caught up to the rest of us. As we grew older we found other measurements, like speed, agility, and strength. Bo and Knapsack became the fastest. Hoops remained the tallest while Gun exceeded everyone in strength. We grew to learn that each of us was special in his own way.

The Castle sat up on the top of the hundred-foot hill. The official prescribed route ran along the street sidewalks. It wasn't long before we found "The Shortcut", which ran directly up the hill. After all, the shortest distance between two points is a straight line (only if the adults didn't tell us to go that way). The problem was that some genius thought it was a good idea to install an eight-foot chain link fence running along the top of the hill, complete with a special kid catching, barbed wire topping. I think they actually installed a pre-rusted fence to save time and money. This left a small space where no man's land ended and a private property began. That was our short cut. The grossly underpaid school administration spent many excruciating hours planning the safest route for us to get back and forth to school so we could totally ignore it.

We would start our climb at the rear of Bo's house as his yard sat at the base of the hill. The angle of the hill was at least 45 degrees and steeper in some sections. The only way to get to the top was to run. The momentum got you past the tough parts. The climb was strictly single file on the narrow path that zigzagged to the top. We did this so often it became an effortless journey. Once we completed the climb to the top where it met the pre-rusted fence, we cut over to the left until we reached the opening, and then backtracked towards the castle. This route was not only vastly shorter, it also gave us more time to play before we left our homes for school. This shortcut worked to our disadvantage as it would give us a false sense of time and inadvertently make us leave too late, and make us run the entire way.

Our classes were divided into two groups during the entire sentence that we were incarcerated at the castle. Every year they would shuffle the deck and deal us out to our respective teachers. We were all never in the same class together because some how they knew that would be a very bad idea.

The eight of us would regroup at the 3:15 bell to make our plans for the rest of the afternoon. We would endure this unofficial ritual for several years, day in and day out. We graduated from third grade and entered the Squire phase.

On September 12, 1962, The Space Race was speeding up when the Soviet Union leapt ahead with the first man in space. President Kennedy quickly responded, "Oh yeah, well we will get to the moon before you so nah, nah, nah, nah, nah."

A month later we almost went farther than the moon, when the world had almost done the unthinkable. The United States faced off with the Soviet Union over the Cuban Missile Crisis for 13 days in October. Remember that Castro guy? Well he became a real pain in the ass. We were kids so we didn't watch the news or read the newspaper. The teachers didn't discuss it in school. Maybe they covered it in the upper grades but eight year olds should not be aware of thermonuclear war and its consequences. We all lived through it and ventured into 1963, which didn't promise to be any better.

CHAPTER NINE

OUR UNIVERSE

*M*y very early morning jam sandwiches usually nause-
ate people. This was the mnemonic to remember
the order of the planets from the sun. It doesn't work
today because Pluto got kicked out for being too gassy.
We didn't care about the other planets, because up until
this point in our lives, we lived in our own three worlds:
Home, School, and Outside. Nothing else mattered.
Screw Pluto.

Home World
Home consisted of two parents and an older sibling
(Bo, Skip, and Knapsack each had an additional sibling, thus violating the 2.5 child law). I do not know if
they ever suffered any governmental penalties for this
infraction. The dads were mostly WWII veterans and
a bunch of quiet but hard working guys. What exactly
they worked hard at was a mystery to most of us kids.
We know they woke up early and were out the door
before we knew it, as we prepared for our own day at
the castle.

There was a deep suspicion that most of the dads
worked for the C.I.A. What else could explain their sudden disappearance in the morning and reappearance
again at 6 o'clock in the evening? They were spies, clear

and simple. They fought the Nazis and the Japs, and were now fighting the Commies. The dads neither spoke of their wartime experiences, nor of their work. I assumed it was some type of secret that they all shared. According to the Rumpelstiltskin Secret Matrix, their secret would have rated higher than a pinky-swear. If they revealed their secret to any of us, there would be an immediate requirement to kill us. We did not inquire.

The moms had previously been in the work force when all the young men had gone off to war. There was a great need to continue with business as usual in America and the women had to replace the men in all aspects of employment. They did an amazing job at keeping the country running with Rosie the Riveter as their poster girl. A funny thing happened when the war was over. Just like that, the women were no longer qualified to work. They put down their power tools and became just plain housewives. This literally meant they were married to their home and couldn't leave it, unless they had to perform wifely duties like shopping for food. If they had a driver's license, many did not have a car to drive. The single car that the family possessed was to be used solely by the dad to get to his secret spy work place.

Women cooked and cleaned and kept house. Divorce was not very popular during this period but when it kicked into full mode in the decades to follow, "kept house" took on an entirely new meaning. The women usually kept the house in the settlement. Comedians later used this joke: Instead of getting married again, I'm going to find a woman that hates me and give her a house. It sounded appropriate.

Staying home with one or more kids was no picnic. When the children are young all you do is fill them with food so they can expel it as fast as they can. Women watched game shows and soap operas on television for vicarious black & white excitement. Sometimes the boredom caused them to find enjoyment in ironing underwear, towels and socks. There was always preparing supper to break the monotony. It wasn't until us younguns got a little older that the women regained their ability to think independently and were able to rejoin the work force. I guess they suffered some type of induced skill amnesia in conjunction with the baby amnesia after the birth of their first child that disqualified them for the job, that they had been doing, and doing well!

Home provided comfort, food, and a place to keep our stuff. Sometimes we even had privacy. Parents taught us manners, to be truthful and respectful of others, even if others meant First-Rounders. Parents basically followed the Boy Scout Oath without knowing it; to help other people at all times, etc. By the time my own children graduated from high school, society had shifted these rudimentary life lessons onto the shoulders of teachers. By the 1990s, it was then up to the school system to teach kids how to behave. This was another great plan like segregation, destined to fail.

Our parents' lesson plan worked fine, with a lot less corporal punishment than they had endured at the hand of their parents. Boomers were not totally without pain, but when it came, it was well deserved. I don't know what the other mothers used for discipline, but mine preferred the dreaded wooden spoon. This was a multi-use tool, used to stir homemade gravy, and then transformed into a ninja-like instrument of destruction. I would hide her collection of spoons under the dining room breakfront out of self-preservation. Somehow, she would mystically pull another from apparent thin air, like a magician's wand, to deal out justice. There was no escape from the stick of death. For special occasions, you might wind up with a yellow bar of soap in your mouth for uttering dirty words.

Our job as kids was to investigate and reconnoiter every inch of our home's interior. I was behind the couches, under the beds, inside closets, up in the attic, and down the basement. I once managed to stuff my entire body into the bathroom sink vanity. I quickly removed myself as soon as I detected a family member entering the room for private purposes, of which I wanted no part. I found every hiding spot to be had. Santa's secret stash was never safe from me. He was really bad as hiding presents.

By the age of nine, I possessed the intricate knowledge of the physical security for this style home and with it, the capability to break into any house in the neighborhood. I was taught well by my parents so I only broke into my own house, and only when it was absolutely necessary. As I stated, we were nine years old, so old enough to be left alone. This meant we were latchkey kids, meaning both of our parents now worked, and they had to give us a key so we could get back into the house. The key made parents feel better so they could leave without guilt. Once in a while I would leave the key that was entrusted to me inside the house and lock myself out. This created the need for what is known in law enforcement circles as breaking and entering.

One time it was not my fault. Honest. I was walking up the front steps getting my carefully guarded key from my pocket to properly enter the front door. I managed to hit the key with my knee as I was adjusting it in my hand. The key floated up into the air, spinning in slow motion, out of my reach. It twisted slightly, enough to drop perfectly in a very narrow slot in between the brick steps. This could not have been accomplished with a million attempts. This resulted in another forced entry.

Besides burglary, we learned a great deal at home. If someone told you the stove was hot, you did not need to touch it *twice* for verification. This concept also applied to wet paint. Touching was not required to verify a sign. A step stool was required to reach a can off a top shelf in the garage, thus avoiding spilling an open can of paint thinner on your face, again. It is not required for you to stick your head between the spindles of a railing to see if it fits. Your head will fit but only going in. It requires special skills and the assistance of others, like firemen, to remove it, to the great embarrassment of your mother. You should not jump down the stairs into the basement, because the invisible cross beam will leave a permanent crease in your skull and probably remove some needed brain cells.

Two very important lessons learned were that interior doors are hollow and sheet rock walls are not as sturdy as you would think. Punching and kicking of these said objects lead to major destruction and the loss of TV for a week.

CHAPTER TEN

SCHOOL WORLD

The school world provided a limitless supply of boring rules and repetitive directions. They did try hard to instill structure into our lives. Over the course of approximately 1600 days, minus some sick and snow days, there were a few days that, let's say, stood out as memorable. On a rare occasion school would be kind of fun. The teacher was rarely the root cause of this fun. It was usually a classmate that would create the artistic opportunity, that would result in banishment to purgatory (standing out in the hall), or worse yet, sent directly to hell (the principal's office) to burn for eternity, or until the bell rang, which felt as long as eternity.

The future Knights would not generally be the driving disruptive force that generated the chaos in the classroom. We had an abundance of assistance from a more than willing group of outliers. The outliers were the group of boys that were not part of the destined eight. They mostly lived outside the Bowl so they did not regularly participate in our after school activities regarding the Forest. At most they visited the Forest for short periods but were not taken with its awesomeness as we were. They did not share in our enthusiasm. They also lacked the camaraderie that the future Knights shared. One major fault with them was that they were "Flat Leavers". They would leave you standing alone at the first hint of a better deal, or any other more exciting adventure, that came along. They would drop you like a bad habit. This was unacceptable. Other outliers were either boogie flickers or sprayers. When the sprayers spoke to you they would project spit onto you. Even saying, "Say it, don't spray it", was not enough to humiliate them. We tolerated the outliers but did not embrace them as one of us.

On occasion we teamed up with the outliers and tested the reserve of the strongest teachers. We held true to the belief that the enemy of our enemy was our friend. When the teacher walked out of the room, all the boys would pile into the large wooden clothes closets at the rear of the classroom, as if she wouldn't notice half the class was missing when she returned. She was surprisingly not amused. We never thought that one through and had no exit strategy. Sometimes she would resume her instructions and wait for us to slither out, dumbasses that we were, back to our seats.

On one historic occasion, Jacob crossed the line with the worst possible choice of an opponent. I obtained this information through school lore because unfortunately I had been with the other half of the Second-Rounders, in the other class. Jacob was in Mr. Hughes' class. Of course we changed it to Mr. Huge, which was more fitting. The guy was a freaking beast compared to even the largest of our group. His hands appeared as if he were wearing catcher's mitts. He was one of those no-neck people. His head sat directly on his torso. There was an unspoken rule: do not mess with Huge. He was generally amiable but you just don't poke the bear. The Big H was one of only two male teachers in the entire school. Teaching was dominated by females for quite a while, thus depriving us boys of upstanding role models. Huge made up for the lack of penii in the school roster.

Most of the time Huge would deliver his message in a low tone and with a smirk of a smile. If the guys were messing around at the science table during math period, he would quietly say, "A in science, F in math." End of discussion.

There is no written record of the actual match that lit the fuse. The rest of story was too interesting to care why. Huge walked towards the immediately sorry offender, as his voice boomed through corridor. Our class was around the corner and down the hall from The Big H and his message came in loud and clear. He grabbed Jacob's school desk with one of his catcher's mitts and flipped it like a coin toss. The desk came up tails, its bowels spilling out on the floor like a freshly gutted deer.

Huge then delivered the coup de grace. He kicked Jacob's gym bag, which had been lying on the floor next to the once upright desk. The canvas bag sailed out of the classroom and into the hallway. The bag picked up momentum on the shiny, battleship gray cement floor. The hallway did not end in a right angle but curved to the con-figuration of the Castle structure. The bag swept the corner as a hockey puck follows the boards behind the goalie. It shot past our classroom door with a zizzing sound, made by the plastic tabs attached to the bottom. That was the cue for our teacher to close the door to our class and muffle the rest of the tirade. She knew the students should not hear this outburst by an adult and she did not want to have to appear in court to provide testimony.

On a less violent day the students were eagerly involved in soap carvings with a lovely young teacher that all the guys had a crush on. As Murphy stated, if something can go wrong, it will. The entire floor was eventually coated with thin soap shavings, creating an indoor skating rink. Bodies were flying haphazardly in every direction. The teacher was reduced to tears, never to repeat this artistic experience again, ever, in her career.

Schools did not have air conditioning so we endured whatever the climate brought. Fortunately the extremely large, wooden, double hung windows opened fully to allow fresh air in. The period architects did not see a need for protective screens on these windows to keep insects out or children in. Safety was not considered an option at the time. When the windows were open, they were OPEN.

This provided the perfect setting on one hot spring day. One by one we constructed paper airplanes and set them free out the window, every time the teacher turned towards the blackboard. Turn, fly, turn, fly, and repeat. It wasn't until the phone rang that we realized our classroom sat directly above the principal's office. When the principal finally gazed out her window from the only air-conditioned room in the building, she saw the entire front lawn littered with crashed air-crafts, sticking nose first into the freshly mowed lawn. I believe the teacher suffered the brunt of the verbal abuse from the boss on this occasion.

My award for favorite performance by an amateur in a classroom setting went to Marty. He absolutely nailed an active epileptic seizure. This was rated far worse on the medical scale than your standard, everyday, ordinary conniption. Marty was not a dumb kid. He was bored with school and didn't learn in the same manner that most of us were accustomed. The education standard of the day was to teach one way and let the kids figure it out on their own. The powers that be finally realized everyone moves at a different pace in the universe and in a variety of ways. You need to teach to the individual student. This epiphany came way too late for Marty.

Marty would throw himself on the floor in his routine, using every inch of his existence, complete with a foaming mouth. The kid had true talent. The teacher panicked, Marty got out of class, game over. A legend was born.

The rest of us discovered much easier and less violent methods to get out of class. One was to volunteer for the chair committee. Since this was a relatively small grammar school, it didn't boast the luxury of an official auditorium. The gym would serve a dual purpose, which gave birth to the chair committee. The sole custodian of the building was a friendly middle-aged Polish gentleman called Ski. This was short for some unpronounceable eastern European name with forty consonants.

Ski's home was a small room off the gym that provided him a small refrigerator and a coffee pot. This was a time before the existence of OSHA (Occupational Safety and Health) and there weren't five thousand regulations to follow. He kept up with the common areas of the school during the day and mopped the classrooms at night, following his own rotating schedule of whatever he felt like doing that night. Ski was a constantly working man, not a hard working man. When it came time for an assembly, numerous gray metal folding chairs had to be wheeled out from storage onto the shiny hardwood gym floor and set up in semi-orderly rows.

Ski was a smart man and proposed to the principal that this procedure would go much faster if the children (boys) were enlisted into a community type service, to assist in the set up process. They would learn responsibility. The chair committee was born. A few boys were selected from each of the older grades to be Ski's assistants. We would all meet Ski at his "office" and receive our instructions, in between sips of his coffee, which included the exact number of chairs and rows that would be needed that day.

The real old guys (8th graders) would be in charge of the heavy racks and roll them out to the gym. The rest of us would unload them from the rack and set them up in almost perfectly straight rows, divided down the middle by an agreed upon space to allow for entry and egress by the student population, and adults, when in attendance.

Before Johannes Gutenberg invented the printing press and mass publication around 1440, the only way to learn how to perform specific skills was by watching how it was done and by word of mouth. The same held true in the 1960s. How else would we have learned about the art of popping a chair? Popping a chair was truly an art form at the lowest level, very similar to farting.

The gray metal folding chairs were both durable yet light and easy to handle and stack. They were purchased in bulk by the Board of Education, for all the schools lacking an auditorium, at a cost savings to the taxpayers of the town. The BOE members had no idea this simple item could be weaponized. The older boys were gracious enough to pass on this secret to the newer members of the chair committee.

To arm the device you must lay the chair on the floor with the seat portion facing down. It then takes only slight pressure using your foot to press the metal of the seat inwards or towards the floor. This creates a very insignificant bulge in the seat that is undetectable to the human eye, when it is unfolded and placed in position for use. The chair is now armed. When the unsuspecting patron places his or her butt on the seat surface, the metal snaps back into the original form making an audible popping sound. It also gives off a rapid vibration. This often startles the user to their feet. I believe, "Oh", is the most common expression of surprise used on these occasions because "shit' would have been unacceptable.

The trick to this technique was to use it sparingly so as not to give away the intent or call unwanted attention from the administration. At most, the group was only allowed to pop a few chairs and spread them throughout the room. Kids are predictable and it was only a matter of time until someone abused this First Rule of Chairdom. Hoops succumbed to the urge and got carried away. He popped over a dozen chairs and left them activated and waiting for the unsuspecting victims.

The student population filed in for the assembly and the fireworks began. Kids were jumping up left and right with loud outbursts. There may have been a "shit" uttered among this group. The resulting meeting of the chair committee was not a fun one. Ski denied any knowledge of this inappropriate action, but how could he not have known. The rest of us received a stern warning from the principal. We stopped popping chairs, at least for the next few assemblies. They weren't going to disband the committee because someone had to set up and break down a couple hundred chairs and Ski wasn't going to do it by himself. It would take him an entire day away from his other chores like sitting in his office and drinking coffee. I told you he was a smart man.

I never reached the legendary status of Marty or Jacob, but I did gain an honorable mention. In fourth grade I was minding my own business at my desk, playing with my plastic ruler and thumb size eraser when, through absolutely no fault of my own, I accidentally launched the two-inch long, pink rubbery object into what NASA refers to as a low earth orbit. Houston, I had a problem. I did not know this was possible (I believe the Military Industrial Complex had not yet perfected this science) but the eraser had pinpoint laser tracking capability. The tiny rubbery craft locked-in on my teacher's ass and then targeted same. The teacher was situated entirely across the classroom and as she bent over her desk it of course scored a direct hit on said target – teacher ass.

I was so uncoordinated at this stage in my life, I couldn't have hit any part of my teacher if she had been standing right next to me, and I was using one of those immense joke erasers that have the saying, "I Only Make Big Mistakes," printed on it. Unfortunately, I did not have a destruct button on my ruler to blow the eraser out of its brief but tragic orbit. The only thing that could have made this worse was if the eraser became embedded in her crack. That would have been called a hard landing. There was no point in denying any responsibility for this dastardly deed, as my face was now a glowing red beacon, to guide lost ships to port, and would have given me up in a heartbeat, so I immediately turned myself in. Try and convince a teacher you weren't aiming at her ass. The entire incident was just a disastrous mission that should have never been launched. Wrong place, wrong time was my mantra. I was banished to purgatory for the rest of the period.

For the most part, our teachers were a nice bunch, for adults. We could tell that they cared about us. Why else would they put up with this crap every day, Monday thru Friday? Some of them were brand spanking new, fresh out of college, and not yet jaded by the system. Some of them looked old enough that they may just happened to have been standing there when they decided to build the school around them. It sure appeared that way.

Our favorite class was gym. There was no homework and you didn't have to study for any tests. We got to change into, way too short, maroon shorts and a plain gray t-shirt, and act like kids. Yes, the community chose the colorless maroon and gray to be the school colors. This artistic pick elicited all the excitement of a cold and cloudy winter day in Iowa.

Our gym teacher was Mr. Zaprillo. We were going to call him Zap (not to his face) until we learned in English class that zap almost qualifies as an onomatopoeia. That was too much information to process.

Mr. Zaprillo ultimately became "The Bird" for some unexplained reason. My best guess is that it originated with the song, *Surfin Bird*. In the song it is clear that the bird is the word. It was certainly a stupid enough reason to call him The Bird. We would sing the song when he lined us up like Marine recruits at boot camp.

A-well-a ev'rybody's heard about the bird
B-b-b-bird, b-birdd's a word
A-well, a bird, bird, bird, bird is a word
A-well, a bird, bird, bird, well-a bird is a word
A-well, a bird, bird, bird, b-bird's a word
A-well, a bird, bird, bird, well-a bird is a word
A-well, a bird, bird, b-bird is a word
A-well, a bird, bird, bird, b-bird's a word
A-well, a bird, bird, bird, well-a bird is a word
A-well, a bird, bird, b-bird's a word
A-well-a don't you know about the bird?
Well, everybody knows that the bird is a word

As he attempted to teach us how to not only stand still, but also line up in some semblance of order, someone would start to sing *Surfin Bird* at the other end of the line, as he reviewed his troops. He would pivot around and rush to the person he believed to be the source, only to hear it from the other end of the line from where he had just run.

The Bird was an adult of undetermined age because all adults were old. The fun fact here is that some of the kids in our class were taller than The Bird. The Bird was the exact opposite of Mr. Huge. I'm sure this is an ego deflator for an adult to be shorter than a grammar school kid, especially a student. His passion was football and I knew he wished in his heart that he were at least a foot and a half taller and 200 pounds heavier. To say he was a hairy little guy is an understatement. His body hair flowed out of his short sleeve polo shirt down his arms and up through the open collar at his neck. He looked like a mini Sasquatch wearing clothes. Aside from these (excuse me) shortcomings, he was totally dedicated to his career.

He taught us remedial sports, such as how to get into a perfect three-point football stance, how to properly hold a baseball bat, and how to do a roll after diving over some of your pals lying on the floor mat. The most important thing he taught us was that we could be children and go crazy after we earned free time to do what ever we wanted to do, close to the end of the period. We chose to play dodge ball, which everyone knows stands for legal brutality against each other. We would wipe each other out with unauthorized strikes to off-limit areas of the body, like your face.

Our favorite game was murder ball. This involved a four-foot diameter, disgustingly dirty, inflated canvas ball. Two teams would converge on the ball crab walking (backs to the floor walking on hands and feet). The purpose was to score a goal, soccer style, by kicking the giant ball. Bodily coordination, what little we possessed, was eliminated with this crab maneuver. We would attack and crawl over each other like ants fighting over a piece of birthday cake dropped on the ground. We would leave the gym, bruised and battered, laughing like maniacs.

Besides taking control of our minds and bodies to mold us into fine, strong young men, The Bird had one other important job. That was to sit in Ski's office and drink a cup of coffee. The two men would sit in the tiny room off the gym and commiserate with each other. The Bird would tell Ski how the students taunt him by singing, *Surfin Bird*, while Ski would tell The Bird how the stupid kids get him jammed up by popping chairs. We loved those guys.

CHAPTER ELEVEN

OUTSIDE WORLD

The outside world gave us entertainment, although we usually had to figure out how to work it ourselves. Outside did not come with instructions. We did not have organized sports complete with flashy team jerseys. We rarely had enough equipment for any one sport except maybe a basketball. It didn't' matter because we always had a great time. We improvised. They could have run an entire Olympic games competition within our neighborhood after we set the ground rules for our own Bowl games.

Since the neighborhood was a half mile oval, the obvious competition was running around it. We ran everywhere all the time anyway, why not around the block. We ran back and forth to school, but mostly back, because we wanted to get home faster than we wanted to get to school, unless we were late, which was most of the time. We ran to each others' homes. We always ran when parents called.

My favorite run was to Bo's house. I would call him on the phone and tell him to hold on. I would then hang up the large black, handset, quietly, so he didn't notice. I would then run out my back door, across my rear yard, clear my four-foot, silver, metal, chain-link fence (eventually without touching it) through the neighbor's yard, cross the street, up Bo's front steps, and ring his doorbell before the phone connection was lost and he discovered I had hung up. That was a challenge we both got a kick out of. This goofy trick made us laugh hysterically every time.

We had the utility pole climb. Telephone poles were installed approximately every couple hundred feet on one side of the street throughout the neighborhood. The poles carried of course, telephone service and electric power lines to the houses. Alas, there was no cable TV service to be had. That luxury awaited us in adulthood. We managed to survive with seven channels that went off the air late at night.

The poles were designed with metal rungs up the side that acted as a ladder so the service guys could climb up them. The utility company was smart enough to only leave nubs near the bottom so stupid kids wouldn't climb up the pole and electrocute themselves. The utility guys carried the missing rung that they attached to the nub. The people that design stuff never take into account the persistence or boredom threshold of the average kid. We also worked as a team and easily circumvented any height obstacle by climbing on each other to reach our goal.

Once we reached the first rung, the rest was a piece of cake. Yes, we were stupid but we had our limits and knew enough not to get too close to the top and become fried chicken. We were familiar with the story of Icarus, who flew too close to the sun. We did not want our wings to melt. We did incur our share of major splinters, as they do not sand telephone poles. Did you ever notice that pole guys wear heavy-duty clothes? They do that for a reason.

One of the best forms of entertainment was delivered directly to our street, without our even asking for it. The neighborhood was only ten years old and someone decided that the entire storm water system needed replacement. My guess is they installed an inadequate system to begin with and it couldn't handle the current flow that exceeded initial expectations. They dropped at least a gazillion, sections of three-foot diameter precast concrete pipes throughout the entire neighborhood. These pipes were large enough for little boys to play in. We only had to duck a little to run through them. We also were able to run along the top of them and hide behind them. We never gave any consideration to the fact that these giant Lincoln Logs could possibly roll and squish us like a bug. Too much fun! I don't think any parents told us not to play on them. They never told us not to play in the street, either. Parents all suffered from the guilt of having ruined the beautiful common open space within the oval.

We tested our skill walking on iron railings that decorated some front steps, climbed maple trees that were planted to make the neighborhood more inviting to newcomers, and staged incredible "fake fights" to imitate the stunts we watched in the latest movies.

Our parents never had to tell us to go out and play. They did have one rule about returning; be home before dark. No kid owned a watch, never mind wear one. The closest thing we had to compare with a cell phone was a toy Dick Tracy Two-Way Wrist Radio that was basically an amplifier. Our parents knew we were out, but they had no idea where we were. They weren't tracking us by GPS because there were no satellites orbiting the earth to receive a signal. Parents made no attempt trying to locate us. Why bother? We were probably fine.

We used every ounce of energy we had to devote to a hard day at play. We had no idea we needed to stay hydrated but we did know that we became very thirsty. After all, it's not like we could carry around a bottle of water with us all day. How dumb would that have been? We were able to meet our needs in another way. Besides the mandatory 2.5 children, suburbanites were also required to have a minimum 50-ft. green garden hose, affixed to an outdoor spigot. There were many of these oases to be found throughout the neighborhood, buried behind some shrubbery.

We had no problem pulling the brass fitting at the end of the hose from the dirt and drinking directly from it. Everyone was well aware that a T-shirt, mostly dirty, could be used as an antiseptic wipe, to remove any hazardous waste from the nozzle to make it safe for drinking. The hose was then passed to the next member and so on down the line. This procedure also applied to soda bottles. The number one rule was, of course, to shut off the water when you were done.

We always became totally involved in the day's activity and surely would have been punished for violating curfew had it not been for our secret warning device. Our climbing-friendly, telephone poles also boasted large streetlights to illuminate the area and keep the neighborhood safe. When the lights started to warm up they would emit a distinctive hum. That sound was our cue to high tail it home at breakneck speed. If we got home after the lights were on, we were toast. Our joke was as follows: Why do streetlights hum? Answer: because they don't know the words. We told it often - a real knee slapper.

The back up alarm to the streetlight was the mom. They would lean out the front door and holler your name in a manner that would make Tarzan's call to the elephants seem amateur. They were totally unfazed at how embarrassing this truly was. The first blast would be you first proper name. The second blast would be your first name followed by your middle name. If they completed the third yell with your entire given name, you may as well run away and join the circus.

When we weren't running, we were riding our bikes. With this rudimentary form of transportation, we were able to carry all our stuff and one or two passengers, depending upon the skill of the operator. Most of the guys had small Stingray bikes that were built lower to the ground. Some modified their bikes by switching to a banana seat, chopper handlebars, and accompanying sissy bar that came up from the back of the seat. These bikes were much cooler and faster than the tank that I rode.

My bike was an adult size red monster contraption, complete with a large center console that housed about a hundred D batteries. The batteries powered the headlight and horn and added a ton to the gross weight of the bike. It had front and rear fenders that I believe came off a 57 Oldsmobile. While everyone was able to jump curbs with their easily maneuverable and lighter bikes, I was resigned to wait for a driveway to make my transition from street to sidewalk. I hated those guys. The only thing I hated more were the show-offs that rode with no hands. It wasn't long before I stripped off all the accoutrements, removed the wheels, and painted the entire thing in a black and yellow zebra design, I'm sure to the horror of my parents, who lovingly picked out this gift for me.

When we rode as a group, we were riding Harleys on the open road, especially after the installation of the specifically selected baseball card. This card was attached by a wooden clothespin to the frame, to strike the spokes as they spun. The card was carefully selected from the shoebox of others because it was not needed to complete the team set. The only thing better than riding was coasting. This activity was usually reserved for downhill riding. It provided the real illusion of riding a motorcycle.

One hazard we often encountered was the dreaded "pants cuff caught in the bicycle chain" scenario. A chain guard would easily prevent this immediate, and most often painful, cessation of motion. Chain guards were metal covers over the chains. They were not cool and thus hastily removed and discarded. We improvised with elastic bands that we removed from the morning newspaper and then applied to our right pants leg. Some guys went all out and used a metal pants clamp. It was a good thing most of our riding took place over the summer months in short pants weather.

The pants cuff entrapment that created an immediate stop action, sometimes led to the dreaded nut-sack collision with either the handlebar stem or the cross bar support that ran from under the seat to the front fork. Rolling on the ground and holding private parts of your body for an adequate period of time was mandatory following impact. This was most likely accompanied by a mournful sound that humans should not be allowed to hear.

Another bike hazard was created by the steel metal pedals that were fitted with teeth-like edges to better grab with your foot. Our bikes were not equipped with hand brakes so foot manipulation was critical. There were times the pedals would get away from us and come around again on their own and catch us with the teeth side hitting us directly in the back of our calves. This would often draw blood and leave a nice wound for display. The guys would never admit that they were spastic and quickly gave the excuse of a dog bite. It didn't fool anyone because everyone knew immediately that you were a spaz.

We played curb-ball using a pinky or tennis ball. Tennis balls were hard to come by as no one played tennis and there wasn't a tennis court for miles. Hop-Scotch and Spud were other favorites. To this day I do not know what Spud means. Ring-A-Levio was a combination of tag and hide and seek but we adapted it to be a much more physical endeavor. We played touch football (also much more physical than simple touch) in the street using telephone poles as our end zone markers. The warning "car" temporarily interrupted street games until the vehicle passed us.

We tried to select a playing field within the street that was devoid of parked cars whenever possible. If there was a car in the area, we used it to our advantage and worked it into the running play for touch football. The QB would give us the play in our huddle of three or four kids. "Cut right at the rear of the Chevy and I'll hit you". We used the parked car as an extra blocker.

No man's land was at the Bud. Bud lived next door to Knapsack and had no kids. Us kids knew just about everyone in the entire neighborhood, even if it was only the last name of the resident. We never knew Bud's last name or anything else about him. He was a Clark Kent type of looking guy that made messing with him scarier than the average neighbor. He wasn't Haystacks Calhoun big, but he was a daunting figure.

We never saw Mrs. Bud and assumed he kept her mummified psycho-like cadaver stored in the attic. Bud's prized possession was a 1960 midnight blue Cadillac Coupe Deville, with a pristine white interior. It was the only Cadillac in the entire neighborhood. We all knew Bud loved this car because he meticulously washed it every Saturday morning, wearing his mild mannered glasses. We also knew that if we as much dropped any type of sports equipment upon said "object of his affection", he would dismember our smelly little boy bodies and comfortably fit all of the parts in his exceptionally large trunk.

It was ironic that we were not the ones responsible for the destruction of the Bud-mobile. Several years later on one cold, snowy, wintry day, a town plow was making a pass in unusually harsh weather conditions. The driver may have been a new employee or temporarily snow blind. Whatever the reason, he misjudged the clearance distance for the plow blade and caught the tailfin of the Bud-mobile, just right. Before the driver realized he had made contact, the blade continued slicing the driver's side all the way to the headlight, essentially cutting the car in half. It looked as if the caddy was a can of corn that had been attacked by a crazed can opener. It was an awesome sight. We really felt bad for the potential serial killer because we knew how much his machine meant to him. When we were all old enough to drive, we all loved our own cars with the same sickness.

The empty space on the opposite side of Knapsack's house (Opposite side of the Bud) was our baseball field.

The field was an unlevel, pothole strewn, rock filled, weed infested mess that sloped down from Knapsack's house and then again to the right towards the Forest. You couldn't pick a worse location to play baseball. It was perfect for us. The pitcher had to throw uphill to the batter. Teams consisted of any boy that showed up of any age. We couldn't be choosy and were lucky if we were able to have enough people to cover the bases, never mind the outfield.

The team on the field was allowed to use whatever gloves were brought to the game, as not everyone possessed his own. Lefties were out of luck. Everyone understood that there would be no sliding on this surface. Sliding would require immediate medical aid. I never agreed with the sliding concept. I believed that if you stopped running and threw your body on the ground, the action of you rubbing your skin off on the dirt would immediately start slowing you down. I never slid.

First base was a large underground flat rock. We scraped the dirt off enough to designate it as a base. Second base was a rusted manhole cover that read Bayonne Iron Works in raised letters. Third base was a broken tree stump. You couldn't stand on it so a runner had to lean his foot on the side of it. The foul area was the Forest off first base, complete with flesh eating sticker bushes. The street completed the opposite foul area off third base. The game usually ended when the "only" game ball was hit into high weeds or into the street and down the storm drain. We often performed daring recovery missions by lowing the smallest player available, by his ankles, into the sewer. There was no volunteering for this mission. It was for the game.

One game ended with a legendary dispute between two outliers. The argument took place at home plate with Jacob still holding the bat. This escalated quickly, far beyond the professional games when the manager kicks infield dirt on the umpire's shoes. Before anyone could move from his designated position, Jacob unleashed his best imitation of Paul Bunyan swinging an axe, and struck Sal in both shins, cutting him down with one chop. Jacob intuitively left the area before Sal could recover. No one felt sorry for Sal. Sal was a dick. The game was abruptly called because to the contrary, there *is* crying in baseball.

Karma did not take its time in dealing out justice to Jacob. On a totally unrelated occasion, a large group was coasting down the street on our bikes from the rim of the Bowl. Jacob was the target to catch that day. Crazy, non-epileptic Marty came up from behind Jacob. He quickly closed the distance between them. The two of them were soon side-by-side racing down the street when the unthinkable happened. Marty stood up on the seat of his bicycle. I told you I hated all the kids that could ride with no hands on the handlebars. I really hated this action but not as much as Jacob was about to hate it.

It is difficult to describe the next few moments. Marty leapt off the seat of his bicycle, cowboy style, onto Jacob, who was still at full speed. The resulting impact created a horrific whirlwind of rolling bodies tangled in with what was left of Jacob's bike. We were all in shock as the pair slid to a stop on the asphalt. We all screeched to a halt just short of the point of impact at the scene of the disaster. Crazy Marty took one look at our faces and he immediately determined it was time to skedaddle. He knew he was about to incur the wrath of the Bowl and quickly retrieved his bike, which had gone on by itself for a bit more, after he abruptly left it. He jumped on it and peddled as fast as he could. This was the last time

Marty visited the Bowl. We assisted Jacob and his mangled bike home. Some things cannot be explained. This was definitely one of them.

One by-product of entertainment was torture. This was not your clever medieval kind of torture: this was plain and simple kid torture. We often tried to measure each other's pain level. One example was a good punch in the gut, sometimes with advanced notice, sometimes not. It was never fun for the recipient if it was a surprise. This also applied to kicking someone in his cookies. This was always painful, but always evoked laughter from everyone but the one on the ground holding his privates.

Giving someone a pink belly required the assistance of at least two other henchmen to hold the victim down so the third can slap the victim's stomach raw. A haircut was achieved by rubbing your thumb harshly up the back of someone's head, starting at the hairline on the neck. A Noogie was similar to a haircut, but administered to the top of the head with your knuckle. A Hemowasi was hitting the person in the throat with the tips of your fingers, where that little notch is, just enough to make them gag, but not enough to kill them. Restraint and control was key in delivering a proper and legal Hemowasi, while avoiding the death penalty.

We would rip the little loop off the back of someone's button down shirt. The loop was called a fag tag, which meant absolutely nothing to us. The loop would never come off clean and leave a significant hole. Wedgies were also popular. This was the action of pulling someone's underpants up their back as high as they would go. An Atomic Wedgie was achieved if you could loop the underwear over the person's head. I believe this was a myth and has never been accomplished. Needless to say there was a lot of damage done to clothing that needed explaining. Moms were not amused by our antics.

We were all experts on not only physical abuse, but verbal abuse as well. Ranking on each other was an art (mothers were off limits). This banter was eventually lost over time through social evolution and kids lost their ability to defend themselves from the now felonious bully. If someone called you a name, you called him something worse. If someone pushed you, you knocked him down. You stood up for yourself and your friends. One rule always applied, you did not hit a girl.

One of the most clever pastimes that we fabricated was refrigerator box downhill. This was a very simple concept born on the day Rhino's family had a new refrigerator delivered to his house. We quickly discovered that we could only sit in this large box for so long before we developed the need for speed. We understood that we needed to make the refrigerator box not only move, but move at a blinding pace. It turned out that we were experts at physics without ever having opened a book on the subject. Living in the Bowl next to a giant hill was most helpful.

Without giving it another thought, we dragged this large object up the hill at the rear of Bo's house. We would have put the ancient pyramid building Egyptians to shame with our efforts. The hill ran at approximately a 45-degree angle and stood twice as high as the surrounding single-family houses in the neighborhood. This was a good day as our entire complement, of eight morons, were present and accounted for.

They say the more the merrier, however this did not increase the group IQ ratio, just the total weight in the box. We carefully selected the best possible launch site. We picked a route that had "fewer" obstacles. Without a moment's hesitation we aimed our vessel downwards. That was the plan, to go down. There would be no trial run with an empty box. That would mean we would have to lug the damn thing up the hill again. Too much work with no fun involved.

We all piled in and... wait. I need to explain that there was a gaggle of eight, eight-year old boys, sitting in a huge cardboard box with not so much as a slit to see where we were going. Not that it would make any difference, because there was no way to steer or maneuver the crate in any manner whatsoever. We are about to hurtle blindly down a steep incline with no other thoughts except to complete our mission, which was to get to the bottom. I knew in my heart that NASA followed a similar checklist. The plan was perfect. I don't recall exactly how we got the momentum going. It could have been by rocking forward until the pitch was just right to overcome gravity. It may have been by all of us jumping in at once and having our mass weight propel the box forward. It doesn't matter because it did move forward, which meant downward.

This was not the Bonneville Salt Flats of Utah and we were not out to set any land speed record. For God sakes, we were in a cardboard box. We weren't stupid! We had no illusions of grandeur. However, you would be surprised to know that a cardboard box can pick up speed quite quickly provided the ideal circumstances. On this day conditions were perfect.

Here we were violating several laws of nature, one of them being collectively stupid, sitting skinny, dumb, and happy in a large cardboard box on a mission to the unknown, in a sensory deprivation craft. We were blind to the lovely scenery passing us by. We could not feel the cool wind through our hair. We could not hear the birds singing outside the box because we were all yelling with excitement at the success of our launch, similar to the group of narrow black tie wearing nerd engineers at a Cape Canaveral blast off. We did not see the large tree that pulled us towards it like a tractor beam catching a shuttlecraft in space as if it were to be pulled into the mother ship. We did, however, feel the impact as mass contacted mass in the most ugly manner possible.

The law of matter dictates that two objects cannot occupy the same space at the same time. The hard facts were that we were the movable object, and a flimsy one at that, with a soft creamy filling, attempting to occupy the same space as a large very unmovable object: an oak tree. Nature always wins out. To put it delicately, our craft was pulverized. Small boy bodies flew in all directions right through the walls of the corrugated cardboard container. The fortunate ones were projected past the tree into sticker bushes, while the not so fortunate came to an abrupt stop against skin eradicating bark. Bodies lay sprawled over the once tranquil hillside. It looked like an extra large dinner meal of Kentucky fried chicken had exploded.

It took several minutes for us to regain our senses, the short supply that we had to start with anyway. We assessed the damage and performed what later became known in medical circles as triage. There were no broken bones, no concussions, some minor bleeding, damaged clothing, but everything seemed just fine. Without hesitation we started to salvage the once proud craft. We collected the remnants and after a moment of silence over the crash site, as the little wheels spun within our bruised craniums, we grabbed the largest pieces and sprinted back up the hill to use the leftovers as uncontrollable cardboard toboggans. Nothing would diminish our fun or our quest for adventure. We were immortal.

In the winter it was almost impossible to climb up the hill after an ice or snowstorm. Down was another matter. We all wore puffy winter jackets with very smooth exteriors. Without hesitation we would dive at the path, head first, landing in a perfect belly flop on the frozen ground. This was the only time I approved of sliding. We would body surf the entire way down. This action provided slightly more control than the refrigerator box, but not much. Too much speed would launch you off course and into a danger zone. The small problem we overlooked was the three-foot high retaining wall at the bottom of the hill. If you were lucky enough to make it all the way to the bottom, you would be catapulted over the wall and become airborne. This launch would create a super belly flop and release all the air out of your body. The moms did not appreciate the extra miles worn into the front of our winter coats that were supposed to last us a few seasons until we grew out of them. The moms did not understand the meaning of fun.

We combined all of our skills: running, jumping, and climbing, to emulate a French military/martial arts form called Parkour. We had no idea we were copying this training because we were kids and enjoyed creating our own obstacle courses for the heck of it. We barely knew where France was. My best guess on how to get to France was that when I came out my front door I would make two lefts and head straight.

We would run any distance, jump over just about anything we could clear, including fire hydrants, your basic four-foot, silver metal, chain-link fence, railings, large four-footed street mailboxes, and an occasion parked car (definitely not the Bud's). Climbing came natural for us except for the time we were scaling the pre-rusted fence at the castle and Rhino got caught up in the barbed wire on top. He hung there like a scarecrow blowing in the wind. It reminded us of the movie, *The Great Escape*, when Steven McQueen missed the motorcycle jump over the fence, while running from the Nazis. Rhino's entrapment was not as dramatic, but we enjoyed watching him for a while, of course not making any attempt to free him. What would be the fun in that? He finally unzipped his coat and fell out of it, hitting the ground with an amusing thud. He then had to climb back up the pre-rusted fence to retrieve the perforated garment. His coat was a small price to pay for fun. I'm sure his mom disagreed.

There were a million things in the outside world to keep us occupied. None of them involved electricity, instructions or warning stickers, which we would have ignored anyway. Before we entered the fourth grade the following fall, we realized there was another world to explore. The Forest was waiting for us with new adventures.

Although West Side Story was the hit musical in 1962, it brought to light the underlying racism in America. CBS dominated the airways with family friendly TV shows like The Beverly Hillbillies, Candid Camera, and The Red Skelton Show as America watched and had no idea life, as they knew it, might end in the blink of an eye.

Chapter Twelve

First Steps

There were only two good unobstructed entrances to the Forest. One was next to Knapsack's house, which was at the end of the row of houses across the street from mine. The area adjacent to Knapsack's house was an open area (our baseball field) but apparently unbuildable or they would have constucted more houses there. After all, space is money. The other entrance was directly across the street from my house to the rear of the Weiner house. The Weiners had opted not to build a fence at the rear of their yard, like all of the inner oval residents had done, because it gave them the appearance of an extended property line leading into the Forest. They were able to use this additional space for their own private use and no one complained about it.

I first started venturing into the Forest through the latter entrance to dump grass clippings. I inherited the job of mowing my lawn because I was born with a penis. Girls did not mow lawns. I think I would have gotten the job even if I had an older brother because I was a Second-Rounder. I would fill our silver metal garbage can to nearly the top with grass, hoist it up over my shoulder, carry it across the street through the Weiner yard, and dump it in the Forest. Today this act would violate several child labor and environmental laws. I would repeat this process as many times as needed until the job was completed. I hated when the grass grew too high forcing me to mow it twice because the mower couldn't handle one pass.

When the grass was damp it would clog underneath the mower and I had to stop the machine and scrape it out, using the dreaded little dog poop shovel. Today there are 47 warning labels on lawnmowers to limit liability of the manufacturer. It's amazing that I never ingested gasoline or poured it in my eyes. Nor did I jam my hand into the moving metal blade of death, and I was just a kid. I survived lawn mowing and took pride in my work because I wanted it to look good. Mowing the lawn is one of the few jobs where you get instant gratification, or amputation depending upon how you do it. I have witnessed the latter and believe me, gratification is a lot less messy.

On my many trips into the Forest, I took mental notes that this was a very cool place in need of future exploration. I have already told you that this was not an enchanted Forest but it was magical. Magical in a way that it insulated us from the outside world. We would come to learn that this special place kept us safe from almost all that was bad outside it's perimeter. We had no clue that the Forest had one miracle waiting for us. When we ventured into the Forest, the world continued to rotate, but without our participation or interest.

I was eventually joined by Knapsack, as his yard was adjacent to the Forest, and it also piqued his curiosity. Knapsack always carried an old canvas army bag around with him. He kept various items in it that he thought he needed, thus gaining his moniker, plus it sounded like his name, Kanakis. Close enough. He always kept a whistle tied to the outside of the bag with a strong lanyard, just because.

Our first discovery was the Gray Rock. This large boulder protruded from the ground, located a short distance into the Forest from the Weiner property line, but not visible from their house. We never really knew how large this rock was but we came to the understanding that it was similar to the Titanic iceberg, with the bulk of its mass lurking beneath the surface. We gave up trying to find out how big it was after a few attempts to dig it up. Why did we try to dig it up? Because it was there! We ended this excavation very quickly. The rock served as our welcome monument to the Forest. We developed our own good luck ritual to touch the rock every time we entered the Forest, as sports teams now hit their banner before entering the playing field. Gray Rock would become a very important symbol to us in later years.

The Forest was pretty much virgin territory, as our country had been, before the settlers arrived and screwed it up. Farmers had vacated the Bowl at least a decade prior to the builders and their bulldozers arrived. This area was most likely unused as farmland given the size of the trees that stood 40 or 50 feet tall. They may as well been Sequoias, as they dwarfed us in comparison. There were no trails but the ground was manageable enough to walk through to create our own paths.

Slowly we ventured farther into the Forest, as our group increased in size and we became bolder. We felt there was safety in numbers. What did we know? We were kids. Our first task was to join the two entrances from Knapsack's house to the Weiner house. It's always good to have an escape route. We did not know yet what evil lurked in the unknown. We were not sure if this Forest had been classified yet as haunted by the Official

Forest Classification Office. I'm sure there is such a thing and it is referred to as the OFCO, because government loves alphabet agencies. It makes them sound much more important.

Our small but determined troop made quick work of establishing negotiable trails that would get more worn and defined with every trip we took. The first roads across this nation followed animal migration routes. Animals have a pretty good sense of direction and don't get distracted by tourist attractions. Early Bison herds that had thundered across the country creating massive primitive highways had ignored this part of New Jersey. This Forest also lacked present day larger wildlife such as deer for some odd reason and the small game such as rabbits and squirrels were not the best of trailblazers. It was up to our own senses to find our way without a mysterious thing called GPS, which was still a half a century away.

Our trails were as direct as possible, only weaving when a large obstacle (Gray Rock) presented a problem. We pushed forward from our original trail until there was nowhere to go but deeper into the unknown. This was a new world to us. This was a nine-year-old's world: 50 acres free from rules, limitations, and adult supervision. We were on our own to explore and stake our claim to this wilderness. We continued our journey until we came upon it. We had not been looking for it and didn't know it, but it was exactly what we were looking for.

CHAPTER THIRTEEN

THE MASTER

W e were well into a dozen explorations before we came upon the discovery. Standing approximately 100 feet from the river was the largest most massive tree we had seen in the Forest. It had an immense trunk that would take almost all of us to circle it with arms out stretched. It was unlike all the other trees that had limbs sprouting high out from their trunks, creating the forest canopy. This tree's limbs originated from the trunk much lower to the ground, maybe only five or six feet high. There was also a natural space at the center of the trunk where all the boughs forked and went their own separate ways. We all knew at once that this tree was the Master of the Forest, because of its size and as we would come to learn later, its geographic location, it sat smack dab, squarely in the middle of the Forest.

There was a wide circular clearing around the trunk. The tree created this area for itself, by not allowing anything else to grow too close to it. The Master would require all the nutrients it could absorb to feed its massive bulk. The Master's limbs hung out high over this private area, clearly defining its own space as if it were pointing to the ground and saying, "Mine." The tree could have been a natural carousel if colorfully painted plastic replica animals were hung from each of the limbs.

The Master would become our base camp, our new home. The trunk begged us to climb aboard and we eagerly obliged. The bark twisted as if a giant had screwed the tree into the ground. This circular configuration in the bark formed natural placements for our hands and feet that made scaling the trunk that much easier. We happily accepted the invitation and scrambled up into the branches. It held all of us comfortably, providing sufficient individual space for all of us to claim as our own. Climbing an ordinary tree is great, but having all your buddies with you in one tree is incredible. We would spend countless hours lounging in our own special tree in the months and years to come. I didn't spend this much time studying for my geography tests. Hence, I still cannot name all fifty states.

We would go directly to the Master (after touching Gray Rock) any time we entered the Forest. If one of us was a latecomer, we would always find the rest waiting for us at or up in the tree. All our ventures would start and end at this point. Once we established this as our new home away from home, we slowly started to move in.

We all scavenged our individual homes for "stuff" that our parents or First-Rounders no longer needed. We collected thingamajigs, doohickeys, and all the what-cha-ma-call-its we could find. Slightly bent lawn chairs that would no longer grace a patio party, a leaky cooler, and pieces of wood that dad would never use or miss, were some of the items that found their way into the Forest.

Although the bark handholds were convenient, a makeshift wooden ladder made life easier for the climb. Wooden planks created a safer and more stable platform high off the ground, within the forks. The décor never came close to luxury accommodations but it was five-star comfort to us. All we were lacking was room service, but we managed.

Our exploration had temporarily come to a halt when the Master was discovered but it wasn't long before we knew we had to continue mapping the Forest. It was our duty and we had only had covered a mere fraction of the area.

It was 1963 and there were now 15,000 military advisers in South Vietnam, wherever that was. Why would they need that many people to tell them what to do? There was something big brewing over there but us kids were still not allowed into the information stream. I did hear that Pope John XXIII died just before we got out of school for the summer. I guess I felt bad but I really didn't know the guy. The world, however, was very sad.

CHAPTER FOURTEEN

A MAZING

The best part of our exploration always started out the same way. On the way out the door, our mothers would call out to us, "And don't go in the woods." First of all, they had no idea that what they called the woods was actually our Forest and second, that was exactly where we were going, every time. I would gather up some companions, or head directly to the Master for a rendezvous. We would then formulate our exploration plan.

The homes that backed up to the Forest stood anywhere from 150 to 200 feet from the tree line. Many of the properties did not have rear fences, but even when they did, there was plenty of room for us to walk along the Forest edge, but still not be on private property. Heading north from the Weiner main entry point was clear all the way up to the northbound lane of the Parkway. We often used this outer route because it was easier to traverse the grassy topography and a lot quicker to get to particular locations at the north end of the Forest.

At the northern point we discovered the most interesting of the Forest's attributes. For some unexplainable reason, a non-native, invasive species of bamboo had taken root and had proliferated to the point of covering approximately 10,000 square feet of the open forest floor. I'm guessing that the construction of the Parkway had in some way something do with this agricultural phenomenon. They possibly threw some seeds down to stem erosion of the land into the nearby river, as it had no trees at this spot, and then the bamboo took off on an uninterrupted growth spurt. It lived and spread unbothered by natural or man-made threats to its existence.

We called this section the Bamboo Jungle. The growth was incredibly thick with each reed about as thick around as a grown-man's thumb. Some of the reeds grew fifteen feet tall. It was almost impenetrable. Almost means that nine-year olds will penetrate it. We had to push our way into the tangled wall with all our scrawny body weight. This was the only way we knew of to blaze a path through the reeds.

In another ten years or so, mysterious crop circles started appearing in wheat fields around the world. These intricate designs were first attributed to alien visitation. It was later uncovered that mathematical pranksters mapped out these designs ahead of time and then walked the fields dragging a board behind them to level the stalks thus creating these elaborate but believable hoaxes. This proved that mathematicians desperately needed a hobby. If we had this knowledge, we would have known enough to drag a board with us through the bamboo to create our own pathways. Not having this information, we dragged each other.

Nothing, however, can deter a horde of little boys from their mission. We devoted many hours to pushing our way back and forth across the bamboo jungle to flatten the stalks. It was not our intention to level the entire field or even make an alien design so as to cause a media sensation and resulting panic. We created a maze for ourselves. As I have stated, the growth was so thick we could create parallel paths less than a foot apart and you could not see the person on the other side. We would spend endless hours hunting each other within our creation. Later on we would also find many uses for this foreign vegetation.

Directly adjacent to the bamboo jungle was another by-product of the previous road construction. The heavy equipment operators chose a spot to dump the excess dirt they had excavated to create a flat surface for the asphalt lane, that would become the Parkway. Most of the area was already flat so they only ended up with several dump trucks full of dirt they needed to unload. It was cheaper to use the neighboring parkland instead of hauling it to another location. They saw no need and apparently encountered no resistance to leaving it on the side of the road. Remember, no one lived in the Bowl yet.

They drove their trucks a few hundred yards off the construction site and instead of spreading it out uniformly, they decided to make one big pile. This, I imagine, was before the birth of the bamboo jungle. They backed up their 10-ton dump trucks to almost the river edge and dropped their loads repeatedly until a 30 foot mound remained.

Years passed and nature reclaimed the dirt by depositing seeds upon it. Soon the mound blended into the surrounding landscape, now as a grassy hill. The bamboo jungle then sprouted at its foot. The hill watched out over the jungle and shielded the bamboo from the river.

The hill was the tallest point of the Forest but offered little assistance as a vantage point because it sat at the edge of the Forest. The trees were too dense to see very far into it. You literally could not see the forest for the trees. We could use the hilltop to partially see down into the maze when tracking our prey during a hunt. It also served as an excellent play spot.

We were able to wear a thin dirt trail up one side and down the other with our bikes. If you didn't keep up the momentum you would be thrown off course and slide down the hill, hopefully stopping before the water's edge. The ride down was unforgiving on both the rider and his vehicle.

King of the Hill was the ultimate challenge. We would race each other to the top on foot and then try and dislodge each other from the summit. This was often not a pretty sight nor was it a sport for the weak at heart. A lot of skin and clothing was lost to the ravages of the abrasive hillside, as the losers would slide to defeat. We would often go home sporting impressive raspberry bruises to be tended to by our sometimes not so understanding moms, always waiting with the Bactine bottle. The cure inflicted even more unsympathetic pain upon us.

One more location we added to our mapping expedition was the island. This island was not your typical island. It was not surrounded by water. It wasn't even near the water. It was a small clump of trees that sat between the bamboo jungle and the Parkway on a small hill in the middle of an open field. It was surrounded by soft wavy grass. This grass was another by-product of reconstructing the area after the road was completed and the trucks were done driving over it and digging up the ground with their immense tires. The contractors were nice enough to grade the entire area to remove the ugly ruts.

The island sat atop a slight slope that emptied out to the river below. It was the perfect spot to lay under the shade of the trees and take a long needed break from hard day's play and adventure, especially a hard fought

King of the Hill. It was in a perfect location to get a nice breeze and watch the cars whiz by on the new toll road.

We almost lost the island and a lot more during one kid-made disaster. Hundreds of thousands of years after man discovered fire, we discovered it again. Fire and kids are perfect together because it's the ultimate toy. Smoking cigarettes was a popular death sport by parents at this time so there were always an abundance of spare matchbooks around that no one would ever miss.

Bo appropriated said matchbook and pulled it out of his pocket as we were lounging at the island. At first it was just the typical flicking the lit match at someone to set him on fire. This was not done to be cruel. It was more of a sportsmanlike challenge like seeing how long you can hold your breath. Neither activity is beneficial to your health. We then came up with the brilliant idea to roll up a ball of dried grass and set it on fire to roll down the hill. Seemed like a great idea for the first couple of balls that withered and went out. What could be more fun than fiery grass balls?

The third one, as they say, was the charm. It had a little too much density and burned nicely. A little too nicely as it stayed lit on its path downhill. It also had a great deal of momentum. The problem was, it was igniting the grass along its path. I said there was a nice breeze at this location but on this day it wasn't so nice. It joined forces with the flaming ball of grass to form an unholy alliance and instantly whipped the ignited trail into a spreading fire that instantly took off out of control.

In the blink of an eye, we had a two-foot circle of fire as the flames raced in all directions at once. One by one someone would start to run away out of panic. Bo took off first because it was his matches. He got about ten feet away but snapped out of it and ran back. Knapsack turned next and then returned. One by one we each thought it was a hopeless cause but we were yanked back by our conscience. We understood it was our duty to stay and fight the rapidly expanding fire. We were stomping on the fire as fast as we could. The circle of fire was now eight feet across. The river was too far away to get water and even if it were closer, we had nothing to gather it up with to pour on the fire. The circle was now ten feet. We were within sight of the Parkway, which meant any minute the State Police would be upon us to lock us up. We were going to get such a beating for this one. I didn't think I would ever watch TV again, the ultimate punishment. I never considered jail. We started taking our shirts off to beat the flames as we continued to stomp on the grass, not thinking we could catch on fire ourselves.

It seemed like forever but we finally got control of the fire and stomped out the last embers. We hightailed it out of there and left a huge black circular scar on the hill. It looked like a small plane had crashed. We didn't return until most of the area had recovered. We learned an important lesson that day. The next time you set a ball of grass on fire and roll it down a dry hill, have water. I do not know how the detective moms did not call us out for our smoke smelling clothes. I'm sure they had their suspicions. They were probably afraid to ask.

While we were worrying about our small burn, there was a racial conflagration building across the county, that culminated in Washington D.C. Dr. Martin Luther King held a civil rights rally that attracted over 200,000 blacks.

On August 28th, 1963, he delivered his famous "I have a dream" speech to the crowd. Our town was mostly white and we had no minorities in our entire school. We were totally unaware of any of these problems, racial or otherwise.

CHAPTER FIFTEEN

FOREST BUTT

We decided to move our exploration to the other side of the Forest for a while until the heat literally died down at the island. As far as we knew, no fire apparatus had been dispatched and no arson investigation ensued. We beat the rap this time. We would not be juvenile delinquents - yet.

Our trans-forest pathways were starting to become well worn and defined with each passage we made. We would also perform routine maintenance by clearing fallen limbs and hacking away a stray bush. It was the wild thorn bushes that would get us while riding on our bikes or running through the Forest. Just when you think you had clear sailing, a half-inch spike would tear through your arm. Every once in a while a clingy vine would rake your face. That was just an indescribable feeling. It was somewhere between a cat clawing you and hot water being sprayed on your skin. We were all good healers so it never left any permanent damage. It did require a visit to the Keeper of the Bactine on several occasions. You think we would have carried our own first aid kit by now.

Our push to the south, just inside the Forest from our misaligned baseball field, brought us upon a new geological formation. It was a great divide in the earth created by a giant behemoth. Ok, it wasn't created by a giant's footprint, but we could dream. It was a ditch worn into the Forest by the water runoff from the development. The builders had run all the storm sewers to empty at one low point at the edge of the Forest. Our guess was that this pipe led directly back to the second base Bayonne Iron Works, manhole cover. There was no need to continue the pipeline any further as gravity would take over at this point and direct the rushing water to the river. In time, the thousands and thousands of gallons of flowing water carved a five-foot deep and about six-foot wide ravine into the Forest floor. This all took place before people began thinking of the environment.

So what do you do with a forest butt crack? You jump over it of course! We scouted out the perfect spot for a running start and a suitable landing area on the opposite side. Our newest endeavor commenced. We would run and jump over this stupid ditch until we were exhausted. The running and jumping was not the hard part. It was sticking the landing or crashing as it may be, on the other side. When we got tired of jumping we would often stand in the ditch and have someone else jump over us. The crack was slightly too wide or we would have used our bikes. This would have moved us past the Bactine stage and gone directly to a free ride in an ambulance.

I'm not sure if this is how Robert Knievel got started in his career. Most people knew him as Evel (not Evil like everyone pronounces) Knievel. He jumped over various things, like busses, riding a souped up motorcycle. EVERYONE always went to see him, or watched him on TV, not to see him make the jump, but to see him crash. He did not disappoint. He had some doozies and broke numerous, if not all of the bones in his body, several times. In 1974 he tried and failed to jump the Snake

River Canyon riding his Sky Cycle. He was a professional nut and idol to all us kids because he had no regard for his own life. It was all about the jump.

We eventually had to abandon our stuntman training ground because we didn't get along with the neighbors. This entire area was always moist, which attracted some unsavory characters. Opossums, one of God's ugliest creations, and rats, enjoyed the comforts of this environment prior to our arrival. The rats lived mostly along the river but usually kept to themselves and we ignored each other. In this particular area, they were more brazen and did not scurry off as quickly when humans were present. We did not enjoy sharing this space so we moved on. The area also smelled most distasteful. This added aroma cinched the name of this location as The Butt Crack of the Forest. We abandoned the ditch and headed back to base camp.

CHAPTER SIXTEEN

THE BEACH

If you followed the Butt Crack to its termination, it would lead you to the beach. It wasn't your typical vacation spot kind of beach. It was more of a sand bar. The river deposited sediment at this point, as there was a natural curve at this location. Storm water runoff hit the area from the opposite direction, coming down from the crack, and flattened the dirt out. The beach was approximately five feet below the bank but usually remained slightly above the water line.

It wasn't a very large area as it changed according to the last storm that came through. It was always undergoing the constant process of building up and washing away. The space was big enough for all of us to stand on it. The beach gave us something else besides a low view of the river. It gave us small stones deposited with the dirt. We would sift through the fine particles of silt until we found the perfect stones. That would be the flat ones. They were good for hopscotch but also were the best for skipping.

Skipping stones was the art of throwing the flat stone sideways at the surface of the water to cause it to bounce off or skip across the water. The trick was to see how many skips you could get from one stone. We would spend hours at this competition. It was amazing we never ran out of rocks. There seemed to be an endless supply.

This location was also the perfect spot to launch any watercraft. We didn't have a boat for ourselves. We would gather anything that would float and set it free upon the open seas. Most often it would be a plastic toy that was at end of life for usefulness. Of course we would laden the vessel with as much fireworks as it could possibly carry before it set sail. Usually a cherry bomb would do the trick. Not only were they semi powerful explosives, they were waterproof.

We would secure the explosive charge to the craft and set the item on fire. By not lighting the fuse to the bomb, we were able to get a bit more float action before it blew up. Sometimes if we were lucky the vessel would burn almost to the water line before it exploded. Destruction and fire were the mainstay to real kid fun. We were careful not to blow up each other's personnel property or one another. We never harmed living creatures and didn't even blow up dead animals because you would have to touch them and that was gross. Amazingly no one lost any fingers.

The beach was almost directly under the Route 22 Bridge. This bridge was much lower than the one that carried the Parkway traffic at the opposite end of the Forest. Because of the curvature of the river, the water was much deeper just past the beach. We could see the bottom along most of the river but not here. The water was a dark ominous shade that warned us to stay away. The bridge also shaded the water giving it an almost black appearance. We were careful to control our stone pitches so as not to launch ourselves into the black water. The perfect water explosion would happen when the drifting article made it under the bridge. The explosion would echo under the structure, which only enhanced our enjoyment.

CHAPTER SEVENTEEN

THE RIVER

Our section of the river that dissected the Forest traveled at a very slight curve. If you were to stand at one end of the Forest at the Parkway overpass, you would not be able to see the entire river as it disappeared around the bend until it reached under the highway bridge. But if you stood at the bank looking at the river, there was an optical illusion that made it appear as if it ran straight though the Forest.

For some reason, we all knew that this river was the border between our town and the other place, no man's land. Just as everyone always asks, why does the chicken cross the road, the answer was the same as to why we pursued our quest to cross the river – to get to the other side.

Approximately a thousand years ago, an Englishman named William of Ockham came up with The Law of Parsimony, also referred to by the cooler name "Ockham's Razor". After all the fluffy stuff is boiled out of this principle, it basically states, "All things being equal, the simplest solution tends to be the best one." Since we did not have the expertise and wisdom of a 13th century friar available to us at the time, we chose, without knowing, the Anti-Razor. (also a cool name)

This method proposes to devise as many plans as possible before choosing the most costly and most difficult way possible. This is the foundation upon which our government is built. We set out to cross the river.

The river was named for Elizabeth, but I have no idea which one. Wild guess is, it was a throw back to merry old England, the home of Ockham. Small world. It measured about 50 to 75 ft. across. Most of the time it sat low from its banks, down about six or so feet from the Forest ground level. This was an indication that when the river was at its full potential storm fury, it would be a deep massive force of thousands of gallons per second, pushing through our Forest. It would be a force not to be reckoned with.

Most of the time it was a gentle rambling waterway that hardly made a sound on its journey. Immediately after a rain storm the water ran brown but sometimes when there was no turbulence, it was almost clear, but never safe. After all we were in New Jersey. Instead of the Garden State on our license plates it should say, Home of Toxic Waste. At this age, we all knew enough not to drink the water, God forbid, or get it on your face. We did wash off our hands if needed and then, not thinking, would touch our mouth and face. Hey, we were kids, not surgeons. Luckily we did not go blind or become mutants.

If we tried once, we tried a thousand times to cross the river. We could have easily walked to either end of the Forest and crossed a bridge. What fun is there in that? Mother Nature had thrown down the gauntlet and we had gladly accepted the challenge. Most attempts were made at the shallowest part where there were some river rocks protruding through the surface. These rocks, we soon learned, were highly polished from the constant erosion from the water cascading over them year after year. I give you this scenario; small boy with great determination + wet slippery rock with Bowling ball type surface + rushing cold water = failure 100% of the time.

We were guaranteed wet sneakers and pants at the end of the day. The really stupid part of this plan was that the visible rock path, if that is what you want to call it, did not extend all the way across the river. If one of us managed not to slip into the water and remain on the impossibly slippery surface, there was nowhere to go. Ockham would have called us idiots and he would have been correct.

We may have devised a million plans for the crossing, from swinging across on a rope (numerous problems with that one, mostly the trees didn't hang over the water far enough) to throwing boards in the water for a makeshift walkway (only to see them float away as soon as they made contact with the water). We thought of installing a zip line or building a rope bridge. There were a few more problems with those alternate rope plans. The only ropes we had access to, were our mothers' clotheslines strung up in the rear yards. The clotheslines often held our clothes that needed to be washed after we fell in the river. These ropes were not nearly long enough to accomplish a crossing. They also were not strong enough to support our weight unless we stole them. Then our mothers would get the ropes back from us and string us up with them, thus proving us wrong on their strength capability.

Yes, we were idiots but we were determined idiots, and it gave us something to do in between our exploration journeys. We never achieved our goal and finally used the bridge after a life altering moment. We did give it our best shot.

Chapter Eighteen

Smoke Dirt

Since we are taking about being idiots, this is the perfect place to tell you about this gem. The Forest underwent changes as predicable as the weather that surrounded it. When we had heavy downpours, we had swampy areas. When there were dry spells, the ground would get hard and crack. Sometimes the rich Jersey soil, famous for growing the best tomatoes, would turn into a dusty desert mixture. We made that discovery this one day.

It was just another lazy summer day. The future Knights were hanging out at The Master with nothing much to do. Everyone knows that boredom is the mother of stupid, and as expected, boredom reared its ugly head. I believe it was Rhino, our designated brain surgeon of the day, who made the discovery, and it was a good one.

Dirt bombs are clumps of dirt that were made by God, on the eighth day, designed for little boys to throw. God was a good guy. Dirt bombs are harmless and explode, in a sense, upon impact with any object, including another little boy. It is up to the boy to provide the sound effects for the explosion because dirt does not make noise. There had not been rain for some time and dirt bombs cannot exist without at least some moisture for the perfect mixture to hold the dirt together. Rhino found a substitute.

He grabbed a handful of dry powdery dirt and heaved it at Skip. It was as if we had discovered nuclear fusion. Smoke dirt was born. The powder not only hit its mark, covering the intended victim, it ascended into the air and lingered momentarily, as if there had been an actual explosion. Skip quickly retaliated with a swift and appropriate response. The United States Military calls this M.A.D. – Mutually Assured Destruction – where both sides lose the battle. Rhino suffered a direct hit. It took mere seconds before everyone was totally committed to annihilating everyone else. It was every man for himself.

The amount of available smoke dirt was limitless in the open 20-foot diameter circle. We soon tired of hitting each other and started throwing the dirt directly into the air. It would hang in the air for just seconds but create a cloud cover that soon became opaque. The genius squad was throwing dirt directly up in the air so that it landed back on us. Elephants use their trunks to throw dirt on their backs in a similar manner to act as a sunscreen. We had no other purpose than to have fun. I can't remember having more fun. It was stupid but fun. This is kind of like adults drinking to excess, knowing there will be consequences, but not caring at the moment.

We performed what appeared to be an ancient tribal ritual until we couldn't throw dirt any more, but mostly couldn't breathe, as we were inhaling the dirt that surrounded us. We collapsed to the ground in laughter. The beating of our clothes with our hands would not suffice to wipe away this joyous celebration. We all headed home still smiling and a much darker shade then we had started out that day but wary of what awaited us.

I walked in the front door and immediately was greeted by "the look". My mother had only two words, "Get out." She had me walk to the rear of the house and strip down to my tighty-whities outside. I don't think she ever asked me how I managed to turn my skin a different color. I had to shake like a wet dog to release any loose particles before I was allowed inside. I imagine this is how Charles Schultz's Pig Pen got started. He was the little boy that created a dust cloud wherever he went. I was the dust cloud. It took three baths to return to my normal state. My mother had to use a cup to gather up the residual sediment left behind in the tub. I guess my mother was grateful this episode didn't result in another trip to the emergency room. But that would be another time.

Our country incurred a grave injury on November 22, 1963 that took many decades to cope with. Almost 190 million Americans suffered the loss of John Fitzgerald Kennedy. Our 35th president was the fourth president to be assassinated while in office. This was the first presidential assassination caught on film. The nation was in shock and then shocked again as his alleged killer was gunned down just two days later on live TV. My nine-year old brain couldn't understand what was happening. The JFK assassination took place on the day of our Thanksgiving Day school play. They closed school the next week as many people sat riveted to their televisions, watching the heart-crushing funeral. The world was sad again and the Forest could not save us from this sorrow.

We had experienced real adult grief and were now ready to become Knights.

CBS called 1963, "The year that everything happened". They were wrong. There was much more to come. It took the death of a president to finally install the infamous red phones in the White House. Kenya achieved independence but no one knew what a Kenya was. Michael DeBakey implanted the first artificial heart in a human in Houston while ironically Tony Bennett left his in San Francisco. Robert Frost died and we didn't know the significance of his death until later.

Chapter Nineteen

It's All Fun and Games Until Someone Loses an Eye

Your parents always told you scary shit, as their own screwed up way to say, "I love you and I want you to be safe." What they really meant was, "I did a lot of really stupid things when I was younger so don't do that because you may not be as lucky as I was." Did we listen? They say, "Seeing is believing!"

The amount of treasures or junk, depending upon your viewpoint, continued to accumulate at The Master. One item that I could have done without was part of a chair. I have no idea who brought it to our Forest home. I do know that it didn't show up by itself because it had no legs. It consisted of just the seat and back bolted to a metal frame. I am positive now that this was the tool of the devil and it wanted me dead. I shall submit my proof.

I came up with a brilliant plan all by myself with no one's assistance. I tied an unused rope to the back of the chair and threw the other end over a lower limb of the tree. Grabbing the loose end of the rope I then straddled the chair. I was a scrawny, maybe 100lbs at the time, but being a kid in the 60s, I was mostly muscle because we never stopped moving. I was able to hoist myself hand over hand on the rope while sitting on the broken chair. I do not know to this day what my motivation was for this act. It is similar to throwing dirt in the air. It seemed like the right thing to do at the time.

I was doing pretty well and making good progress with my ascent. That is until I reached what I believed to be the maximum height I wished to achieve. That would have been approximately 10 feet off the ground. Do not ask me why, because I have asked myself this question a million times, I decided to let go of the rope. I really didn't think this one out to the end game. Gravity has been, and continues to be, my mortal enemy, and did not disappoint me on this very day.

I not only plummeted, I rotated slightly to make a perfect landing on my back, a reverse belly flop, if you will. This type of impact forces all the air out of your body as if someone jumped on a rubber hot water bottle. I was the hot water bottle. Surprisingly I was uninjured, or didn't notice if I were, because I could not breathe. I was gasping as if I was drowning and tried to suck in a morsel of air. Nothing was happening. Of course my friends did what friends do. They laughed because this was hysterical. I would probably have laughed if it weren't me sucking wind. All I wanted to do now was breathe. We really take this breathing activity for granted.

It seemed like an eternity but finally something clicked and my respiration system began to function properly again. This truly scared the crap out of me. I had never thought about death, especially my own, until that moment. I was only a kid and I realized I could die. This was not a comforting revelation. I had to sit and recover for a while before I could rejoin the group. I did not relay this event to my parents, as I knew I would be restricted from reuniting with my friends, like a parolee forbidden to associate with other felons.

The chair from hell was not done with me yet. Days later someone improvised on my very stupid plan and tied the rope to the upper branch to let the chair swing freely. This was a much better idea, something we could use for entertainment. Everyone took a turn on the new swing.

Maybe I fell harder than I thought, as I was not paying any attention when it was Hoop's turn on the chair swing. I was walking past the area with no mind to the large moving object and he caught me right in the face with the edge of his sneaker, knocking me back. I instinctively grabbed my new injury and immediately felt a wet sensation. Blood was streaming down my face from my eye area. Bactine was not going to save me this time.

Hoops offered to walk me home, maybe out of guilt, but it was totally my fault for entering his restricted flight path. It seemed like a very long walk and I bled the entire way home. Surprising, I wasn't crying or upset. I was no stranger to hospitals and knew that was my ultimate destination. I'm thinking now that it must have been a weekend because I knew both my parents were home. I walked in the front door holding my face and asked loudly, "Whose turn is it to take me to the emergency room?" My father was immediately volunteered. My mother had her share of trips and it worked out better this way because he had served on the local ambulance squad and wasn't the least bit squeamish, not that my mother was. She won the chance to take me to the ER on several other occasions including the one when I bit a hole in my tongue. On that occasion I was racing my older sister up the wooden basement steps and tripped, landing on my chin and driving my top tooth into my tongue. Boy, talk about blood. That was a real gusher.

This time we entered the ER with my head wrapped in a blood soaked towel. I love when they ask you what the problem is. I wanted to say, "I think my towel may be bleeding to death but how about you take a guess." I was finally escorted to the inner working area. This very nice Japanese doctor met me in the procedure room.

I immediately hoped that my dad had not previously met this doctor under wartime circumstances. I pictured them both in a hand-to-hand fight to the death on some remote south Pacific island. All of a sudden the siren sounded alerting everyone that the war was over. The two warriors backed off and called it a draw.

There was no aha moment, of recognition between them so I assumed I was good to go. They had me lie down on the table and I guess they administered a local anesthetic to my swollen face. I did not feel anything after that, but I was wide-awake during the entire process. I was taking mental notes. The doctor then proceeded to stitch up my eyelid, as he whistled. I was looking up through an extremely swollen face at a smiling Japanese man who at one time, may have been my father's mortal enemy, as he sewed my face back together, and he whistled while he worked, like one of the seven dwarfs. It doesn't get better than that. When I returned to the scene of the crime, I cut the swing down and threw the chair in the river. There would be no third attempt on my life. Fool me once, whatever.

I healed with no complications and we survived the rest of the summer with only minor kid injuries. The summer seemed to fly by doing pretty much nothing but hanging out with each other. Sometimes we would just sit in the tree and talk about a television show or a movie we had seen. We couldn't memorize the dates of significant battles in the Civil War but we could recite an entire two-hour movie verbatim after only having seen it once. This would include sound effects and stage directions. That was pure quality time with friends.

The nation's spirits were lifted again in early 1964 with an invasion by a small but skilled special ops team. It was not pay back for the Bay of Pigs nor was it a hostile coup. It was a social evolution. The Beatles landed in New York City on February 7th. Nothing would be the same after that. Music, clothes, and concerts, everything, including the length of our hair would change.

A couple weeks later, some guy named *Cassius Clay* beat Sonny Liston for the World Heavyweight Championship. Clay and the Beatles were strangers from two different continents that would eventually unite against the spreading black cloud that was Vietnam.

CHAPTER TWENTY

THIS WAS NOT ALICE'S RABBIT HOLE

Every spring the Parent Teacher Association (PTA) would hold a fund raising fair at the Castle. I had no idea what they purchased with this money, nor did I care. The fair was always inside the gym without a thought to moving it outside, where they had to contend with unpredictable Jersey weather. It was also easier to control the gate attendance and everything could be set up ahead of time. There were various booths with games and contests of skills. One standard favorite with the kids that appeared on an annual basis was the ping-pong ball toss. The player would stand behind a barrier, most often a collapsible, wooden folding table, and toss a ping-pong ball into a small goldfish Bowl. The Bowl was half full or half empty, depending upon your outlook on life, and contained surprisingly, a goldfish. Who saw that coming?

If you were lucky or unlucky enough, depending upon your view of goldfish, to land a ball in the water and scare the little fish shit out of the poor creature, you got to take the Bowl and the fish home for your personal viewing pleasure. Adults knew that transporting a swishing glass Bowl of water home by a kid was nearly impossible so they placed the traumatized little fellow in a sealed plastic bag (the fish not the kid). This was so much more comforting. The fish, often named Goldie for some odd reason, was released back into the wild when the child returned home. The wild was actually the same small glass Bowl that contained about enough water to make a large cup of coffee.

Experts (Google) say, *the average life span of a pet goldfish is five to 10 years. In the wild, (not a cup of coffee) they can live as long as 25 years. In fact, the oldest goldfish ever recorded was 43 years old. But prolonging the life of your fish depends on proper care and tank environment.* So, in reality terms, these goldfish were lucky if they lasted about a week, because that's about how long it took for a kid to forget to either change the murky water in the coffee cup, or feed the damn thing a mere sprinkle of the most God awful smelling fish food. The odor was so bad that you couldn't get the little red plastic cap back on the container fast enough before the stink would permeate the entire room. I have a strong belief the substance was Soylent Green. In essence, the favorite and exciting ping-pong ball toss was a game of impending death for all the Goldies at the fair. Disposal was easy enough with a simple wave goodbye and a flush.

Other family pets would find their eternal resting place pushing up daisies in the pet garden. They included but were not limited to; hamsters, gerbils (basically the same thing), snakes, frogs, birds, lizards, turtles, and a rare exotic thing like a skunk. We went through a lot of different pets in our home. I think it was my aunt that brought me a pair of white mice that had been recently pardoned from lab experiments. The mice were so adorable. That was up until the moment they chewed their way out of their cardboard box and we had to hunt them down as if they were fanged, rabid killers.

It is very disturbing to see your pet caught in a trap that pretty much cut it in half by the unforgiving metal spring loaded bar of death.

My mother had a blue parakeet named Pretty Boy. She taught it to walk around and climb on her hand. That's about the extent of our animal training skills. Pretty Boy sat in his spacious wire cage in our small kitchen, watching the family activities. That was, up until the tragic cooking incident. There was a great deal of preparation for a big holiday meal that year. Everyone had a job to do and the ovens were running all day baking cakes and roasting meats. No one noticed the temperature of the room because people were moving back and forth between rooms. Heat has a scientific tendency to rise and it did, exactly to the level of Pretty Boy's little home that was hanging from the ceiling. He finally succumbed to the drastically changing environment, clutched his little chest, and dropped off his little perch, dead. That was our last bird. It also put a damper on the holiday.

Larger pet deaths posed a more difficult challenge and soul-searching reckoning with the hereafter. All the future Knights possessed, at some point in their kidhood, a myriad of pets. Many kids had the obligatory point five (.5) dog, as required by the United States Census Bureau. These creatures were members of the family and most difficult to flush. This would require an immediate visit by the plumber to rectify the ugly matter. Seriously, Rover either was hit by a car or got old and disappeared to the dads' mysterious, hidden C.I.A. "Farm." Dogs and cats rarely ended up in the backyard graveyard next to the tomato plants.

Now you are saying to yourself, "This ass hat tortures and kills small animals like a beginner, serial killer in training. What the hell does this have to do with the Knights?" Keep your shorts on because I'm getting there.

My father found an apparently abandoned baby bunny, maybe only three inches long out in the garden. The good news was that he didn't mow it. The bad news was that he thought we could care for it until it was big enough for it to return to nature. Well it returned to nature a lot faster than any of us thought possible. I discovered its stiff little corpse in the box home we had created for it in the garage, the very next morning. I picked it up and brought it inside to show everyone the very hardened creature. This was met with vast disapproval along with contorted faces and a great deal of pointing. I was directed to return the once cute bunny, now technically a paper weight, to where I found it.

The only thing left to do was to perform a proper burial. I grabbed dad's sturdy metal shovel with the nice green handle and headed outside. During my preparation I reasoned that I did not have to add bunny to the pet garden; I possessed an entire Forest. I picked up Knapsack on the way. He was able to obtain his own shovel. We had a plan. The Master seemed like a perfect spot because there was a clearing away from the other trees that would make digging easier for lack of roots.

We only needed a hole large enough to place the shoebox that contained baby bunny's rigor mortised remains. That would not take long at all. The digging went so well that we easily surpassed our goal of a shoebox size hole in no time flat. We kept on going, and going, and going. It wasn't long before we were standing in a substantial pit. We kept digging. Why not? All thoughts of the decent burial were lost as was the small shoebox that contained the poor bunny's remains in an eternal running pose.

As it was on other days, one by one, the other future Knights arrived. They asked us what we were doing as if it were not obvious and we told them that we were digging a hole. They did not ask why. They understood. They were all excited to jump in and help so we rotated out of the hole. The hole grew bigger and deeper with every new change of shift. We all worked for the rest of the day until it was time to go home. For the life of me, I do not know why but the goal of every child was to dig a hole to China. We had been warned on several occasions when we chose not to eat our vegetables that children in China were starving. I guess we would learn the reason why when we got there. We were well on our way.

The next day we all returned with shovels and other implements of construction, like we were heading to Fred Flintstone's quarry, except that our Yabba-Dabba-Doo moment was not when the foreman pulled the bird's tail at quitting time. Our excitement started when we arrived at the hole and continued the project as if we knew that was our mission. The hole grew larger over the next days and weeks to come. We paused when it looked like a really deep grave because it was difficult to get out of it. For a few days it was just a trench about six feet deep. We jumped over it for a while, because it was there and it didn't smell like the Forest Butt Crack. We didn't have a ladder to dig any deeper so the next option was to dig sideways. We dug.

The hole finally reached an agreed upon completion dimension that would comfortably have accommodated a full size Chrysler Town & Country station wagon, if it were lowered in by a crane. The roof of the car would then have been level with the ground. It wasn't just a hole anymore. It had style. It had a built in stairway so you didn't have to climb up the sides. It also had an extended fireplace area with a chimney to release the smoke. Yes, of course there was fire involved. If you're going to dig, you may as well dig with a purpose.

Similarly, in another point in history, President Theodore Roosevelt was ultimately given credit for linking the Atlantic and Pacific Oceans for a shorter trade route, when in fact it was little Juan Carlos who started the project. His pet Spider Monkey met with an untimely and premature death. Juan gathered up a group of his closest friends to inter the deceased creature. As it happens with little boys, the group got carried away with the burial and the Panama Canal was born. Unlike Juan, we knew when to stop.

We moved all the extra doodads that were not firmly attached to the Master into our new subterranean home. The excavated dirt surrounded the hole, making the hole to appear deeper than it was. This was remotely similar to the castle illusion. We literally enjoyed our new "digs" but it was missing something. We continued to customize it with nooks and crannies for specific storage purposes. It still needed something but what was it?

A roof! It dawned on us that our shelter needed to be enclosed. The Bamboo Jungle answered the question, "How?" We constructed a makeshift frame over the hole with old 2x4s nailed together for the proper length. We added support columns in the center because the hole was too wide to allow a freestanding roof. We then conducted material runs back and forth to the Bamboo Jungle to supply the required roofing material. The longer shoots would reach across the width of the opening across the support boards. When it was completed, the once destined bunny grave had been transformed into an authentic looking, Burmese tiger trap, minus the pointed sticks entrenched into the ground to impale the hunted prey. We had no desire or need to kill a tiger. We were in Forest Heaven.

CHAPTER TWENTY-ONE

THE TREE MAN

W e had mastered the art of back and forth because we were kids. Kids never walk directly to anywhere as demonstrated by our daily treks to school. What may have appeared to be random wandering was actually, in our minds, walking with a purpose. That exact purpose did not have to be stated and could be determined at a later time. During our wanderings, sometimes we brought misery and danger upon ourselves and sometimes it found us.

All eight of us were present this one day so we set out walking near the edge of the Forest, closer to the property line. I do not recall if we were headed back or forth at this time. Like Chuck Berry, we had no particular place to go. We walked in single file as usual. It was against outdoor etiquette to walk as a group. We mostly walked in silence because we were guys and there was no need to talk, so we didn't need to be next to each other. The trails were very narrow and we didn't see any good reason to make the trail any wider.

As if someone gave the order to halt, we stopped in step, mimicking a trained marching band. We had all felt an eerie presence among us. We scanned the surrounding Forest without uttering a word. We had no idea what it was we were looking for. The eight of us scoured every bush and tree, looking for the thing that had unexpectedly grabbed our attention. The unknown presence had made the hair on the back of our necks stand up. Our eyes eventually wandered up into the treetops because there didn't appear to be anything at ground level near us.

There, on a sturdy branch, about 20 feet above us, was a large manlike figure covered in leaves. It was a man but there was something strange about him as there was no sound of leaves rustling when he moved. The leaves appeared to be a part of him. No, it was his clothing. He was dressed head to toe in full camouflage, complete with a similar camouflage mask that totally obscured his face. That was not the disturbing part.

What really caught our undivided attention was the fact that he was holding a large bow, with an arrow positioned and ready to fly in our direction. There is a human characteristic that has enabled mankind to survive throughout history. It is called the fight or flight reflex. When sensing danger, a normal human being experiences this reflex and either moves forward to fight the threat, or runs in the opposite direction to escape it, and live to fight another day. We did not choose to run at this Tree Man for several reasons. He was in a tree. He was big. He had a weapon. It was aimed at us. We were not total idiots. The key word here is total.

Both our fight or flight reflexes were semi-retarded so we stood there. I believe the expression is, "deer in the headlights" syndrome. We waited for Tree Man to make the next move, which may have been to decide which one of us he was going to pierce with what now appeared to be an immense arrow, and then mount on his cabin wall. He slowly released his finger pull on the draw of the bowstring. He then began to climb down from his perch. This was our chance but we still did not flight. You know what I mean. We were not normal human beings.

The Tree Man approached us. He was not as intimidating on ground level as he was standing above us, but he was still a presence to be reckoned with. He slowly peeled off his multi colored, nature coordinated mask to reveal Dofort. Dofort was not a maniacal killing machine. He was worse. He was a man-size First-Rounder, in OUR Forest! He was scary with or without his camouflage attire. He was four years older than us and he was also, unfortunately, in my sister's class.

He told us he had come to hunt rabbits. I wanted to bring him the little stiff bunny, that was the catalyst for the creation of the underground lair, but it was lost under the mounds of excavated dirt. Besides that, we didn't care why he was there, we cared that he was there. We quickly changed the subject from, "You stupid shit, you almost impaled one of us to a tree" to "This place is totally lacking any sort of wildlife and it sucked and we were just leaving." We walked out of the Forest leaving Dofort (forever to be referred to as The Tree Man) standing alone. We never looked back to show any type of interest in him. We hoped he would take the hint and act like the Tree Man that he was and leave. The last thing we wanted was for him to stumble upon the Master and our underground lair.

We lucked out on this occasion. We believed Dorfort was truly an outlier. He was a First-Rounder, who generally had no interest in our Forest. He also lived far enough out of the Bowl that it was an effort for him to make the trip. He left behind The Legend of the Tree Man. With each telling of the story, the Tree Man grew larger and scarier.

The Legend

One cold Halloween, a storm was brewing but there was no rain. It was an incredible electrical storm with numerous cloud-to-ground lightning strikes. One bolt found its mark, sending a billion volts of electricity into a rotted tree. Instead of exploding on impact, the once beautiful tree absorbed the energy creating petrified remains, giving it new, more powerful life than it had ever had before. The tree slowly took on a human form. The Tree Man lived. It was able to use two large limbs as arms. The straggly branches formed hands with long prickly fingers. It stepped out of the ground where it had stood for decades dragging its roots along with it. It hated people because of the suffering it had endured over the years. Man had torn its branches off for firewood and carved their name in its trunk. It wanted revenge. It constructed a bow from one of its branches and created arrows from the bones of the last boys it had slain. The arrowheads were carved from his victim's teeth. The Tree Man wandered the Forest in search of new prey to fulfill its need for revenge.

The best version included a mass impaling of three boys at once, with a giant arrow fired from a tree slingshot. We loved to tell this story to the younger kids in the neighborhood. It kept them out of our Forest and kept their parents awake all night as the children relived the story in their nightmares.

CHAPTER TWENTY-TWO

KNIGHTHOOD

Our group had been together for half our lives. We really had been together for our entire conscious lives. We were 10 years old but had accomplished so much in the past five. The encounter with The Tree Man was our wake up call. We had faced possible death (had it been the real Tree Man) and did it together. We didn't blink in the face of danger. We really didn't do anything, as I had stated; we were deer caught in the headlights. No matter. The Tree Man, without knowing it, gave our lives purpose and we all felt the need to immortalize this moment in some way.

We hid and waited and watched as Dorfort finally exited the Forest, carrying his instruments of death. We circled back into the Forest through the other entrance. Our destination was Gray Rock. The Master was our home base but the rock acted as a significant monument to the Forest. We had designated it as our good luck stone from the very start and had already touched it a thousand times every time we entered the Forest or passed by it. We were all still alive so we reasoned that our lucky charm must have been working.

We circled the rock as if it were an altar. In essence, it was to us. We weren't there to celebrate a religious ceremony or make a sacrifice. We were there to commemorate our friendship. We needed a name to call ourselves. We weren't a gang. We were more than that. We were as close as family and devoted to each other. Skip was the first one to see the significance of us standing in a circle. He said, "Knights of the Round Table." It immediately sunk in with all of us. Hoops commented that we didn't have a table. I said, "We didn't need one" and the Mechanic said, "Just Knights." Rhino added, "Of the Forest." Bingo. Everyone agreed. We were now and from ever forward the Knights of the Forest!

We didn't need a king to serve. We were there for each other as equals. We basically lived with each other except when we went home to sleep. We knew each other's families and fought with the other guy's respective siblings like they were our own. We walked into each other's houses without knocking and were welcomed to do so. The doors were never locked. We called each other the worst of names that a ten-year-old kid could think of, and laughed about it so hard we cried. We physically tortured each other and often said hello by punching each other in the arm as hard as we could. This would create what was referred to as "dead arm", because it was pretty much useless for a while. We were truly brothers and now we had a higher purpose. From this moment on we would watch out for each other in any way we could. We stood up to the Tree Man together and nothing could stop us or harm us again. We also would protect the Forest as our second home.

Tommy Gun was the first to bend a knee at the rock and place his hand upon the rough edge. "Knights", he said. We all joined him surrounding the rock and placed our hands on top of his. One by one we uttered the word. "Knights."

We had never entertained any thoughts of this group not being together. There was never any reason to doubt that our time together would ever end. We were kids and never knew anything else but being with our friends and being in the Forest. Unbeknownst to us, there would come a day in the far off future, that we would not be able to recall the last true day that we had all played together. That special memory would fade as a cloud dissipates when the sun smiles down upon it. Those unimaginable thoughts would not enter into our minds on this triumphant day. On this day, there was hum in the air. The streetlights were sending us the warning signal. It was time for us to leave the Forest. This time we left as Knights.

CHAPTER TWENTY-THREE

THE LITTLE BIG HORN

There are times when The Tree Man attacks you, and then there are times when nature totally throws you under the bus. Another beautiful day in the Forest was an excuse (not that we needed a reason) for one more hike. Most of the time we stayed true to the trails that we had created from one location to another. On this occasion we decided to stray off course because we felt like it. We had no rules. All the Knights were accounted for except the Mechanic. The poor guy was undergoing a torturous ritual better known as shopping with you mom. Boy, were we were going to give him the business over this one when he returned.

We started out from the Master and headed towards the Beach. The usual path was to hug the bank of the river as the most direct route. We didn't feel like being direct so we curved back to the center of the Forest then looped right, as if our destination was the Forest Butt. We then cut directly through a relatively small open patch of straw grass. We hadn't gotten halfway across it before we realized we were in serious trouble. I remember the famous words of General George Armstrong Custer when he said, " Did you hear something?"

A single bee had landed on Skip and he nonchalantly swatted it away. We were accustomed to bugs landing on us all of the time. Another landed on Hoops and he did the same. One by one, bees began to set down upon us as if we had become the designated landing zone for a disoriented squadron of bees. The touchdowns rapidly increased in number while the microseconds between the landings diminished. We were soon swatting ourselves all over our bodies. We transformed into a gaggle of whirling dervishes. Our spinning and hitting had no impact on fending off the feverous attack of bees. It was as if we were the Pony Soldiers and had absent-mindedly wandered onto the Little Big Horn. This, my friends, is what they refer to as a curmudgeon kerfuffle. Some others would have referred to it as a shit storm.

Hoops yelled, "Run!" We had unknowingly disturbed at least one, but I'm guessing a huge cluster of yellow jacket nests, where they had carefully burrowed out of sight. We instantly obtained a thorough education on yellow jackets during their subsequent attack. Apparently these satanic little insects are ground nesters. They are a very social bunch and their colonies can contain thousands of insects at a one time. I said they are social. This does not make them friendly (Ted Bundy was social to promote his agenda of murder). On the contrary, they are sons of bitches, especially when a bunch of ass hat boys step on their house, endangering their queen.

Yellow jackets are not bees but are actually wasps that can be identified by their black and yellow bodies (gang jackets). The truth is that the yellow jackets thought the wasps were too wimpy so they got their own colors and formed a new gang that totally kicked all the other bee gang asses. If all the other bees were either the Jets or the

Sharks in West Side Story, then the yellow jackets would be the fucking Nazis on steroids that not only killed Tony, Bernardo, and Riff, but they would wipe out both gangs and their families, and then come back, kill Doc just for fun, and burn down his soda shop. Yellow jackets sting you just for the hell of it. Then they call their friends over to get a shot at you. That's where the social part comes in.

We also learned about the physics of movement that day. A yellow jacket can fly between 20 and 30 mph. Make that 35 mph when they are really pissed and on a seek and destroy mission. The fastest man that we knew of at that time was Bob "Bullet" Hayes. He had one of the fastest 100 meters times playing for the NFL. Everyone wanted to be Bob Hayes. We sincerely wanted to be Bob Hayes at this very moment. Unfortunately we were not trained super adult athletes. We were awkward, prepubescent, uncoordinated kids with two left feet. We were lucky we didn't suffer a fatal injury getting dressed in the morning. Even if I had been Bob Hayes, I could have only sustained his incredible speed for a short burst before puking up my morning Cheerios. I also had to maneuver around a myriad of Forest obstacles while I cried. The jackets can sustain their speed for up to a mile and I swear I thought I heard them laughing at us during their pursuit.

They say when a bear attacks, you do not have to out run the bear. You only need to be faster than the last guy. When you are attacked by a swarm of bees, excuse me, wasps, you are basically fucked because they outnumber you a hundred to one and they can hit you from multiple angles. They were dive-bombing us like Kamikaze pilots after an all night Meth binge. Another pleasant fact is that these little buggers retain their stingers so they can each sting you multiple times. They were more than happy to come back for seconds and were so inclined to do so on this occasion. I guess it was a slow day at the hive.

We ran through the Forest as the large cloud formed a big scissor while they pursued us. I didn't turn around to see this but I have witnessed this in many cartoons so I know it to be true. The head of the yellow jacket gang smirked with his stupid wasp face and called off the attack as we reached the edge of the Forest. Their turf was safe and they had done their job to protect their family. They had inflicted significant damage upon our group except for the Mechanic, who was suffering shopping with his mom. He won that day and would not be verbally tortured by us. He got the last laugh that day.

We each had multiple stings all over our bodies. We were unfamiliar with the term anaphylaxis, which is a severe allergic reaction to a single bee sting. This could be a potentially life-threatening condition to some people. We luckily found out that we were, fortunately, not some people. I think we may have overdosed on Bactine that day. We all suffered the predictable warning from our moms, "Don't be playing in the woods." We weren't; we were playing in Our Forest. We designated the straw grass area as a no-go-zone and totally off limits. We learned ever so slowly.

Chapter Twenty-Four

Defense of the Realm

S kip had found a book on Knighthood and wrote down Knight's Code of Chivalry and Vows of Knighthood for the rest of us to read. There was a lot of good stuff for us to emulate but the one rule we embraced was about not fearing your enemy. This one struck a cord with us.

We had dodged a bullet, or in this case, an arrow by the Tree Man. Our Forest would have been ruined had Dofort lumbered into our secret lair. We hoped he would not return but we knew hope was not enough to protect our Forest from interlopers. We needed a plan. We needed to arm ourselves for battle.

Beside self-destructive activities, we had a penchant for creating hazardous items. We could turn the most harmless item into a lethal weapon like a face-eating chair swing. A ballpoint pen became a spitball launcher – child's play. We had already experimented in launching a paper airplane out of a classroom window. We discovered that when you add a pin to the nose of the plane, it becomes a guided dart, capable of sticking into a drop ceiling – creative. An aerosol can could easily be turned into a devious flame-thrower. We had not had a lot of luck with fire so we scrapped that idea immediately. It made no sense to destroy our home to protect it. There would not be a scorch the earth policy.

One other item we took off the table was introduced to me on a family visit with my distant cousin living in Virginia. I learned some really serious shit on that trip. Apparently they are really bored in the country and take destruction to a much higher level than plain old Jersey boys. As we played out in a small wooded area behind his home, we of course started a small fire. This was apparently a mandatory boy thing. Everything appeared normal so far. It was more of a campfire than the usual out of control wildfire that I had heard rumor of starting by accident on occasion. This fire was built in a self-contained pit.

Cousin Einstein takes a palm size CO_2 cartridge used to make seltzer, later used by some for inhaling and getting high (what didn't they use to get high in the 60's?), and tosses it into the fire while yelling to me to dive behind a strangely convenient makeshift wall of boards adjacent to the campfire. I didn't know why, but I instinctively followed his lead without asking questions. I cleared the barrier just as the metal cartridge exploded, sending little jagged pieces of shrapnel flying into our barely protective bunker. The freaking asshole almost killed me with a homemade hand grenade. The Knights were not yet prepared to declare total warfare back home.

I believe what became our most ingenious creation had been passed down to us from an older sibling, the enemy. It was truly ironic that we were planning on possibly turning this information against the First-Rounders. We obtained several lengths of copper tubing and cut them into three-foot sections. We then filed down the rough edge and duct taped it for safety. Yes, we were concerned with safety while fashioning home made weapons.

This once harmless plumbing article was transformed into a deadly accurate blowgun. The darts were constructed by forming paper cones to fit the diameter of the tube. We then affixed a meticulously cut and filed piece of a wire hanger as the spike to the cone. This was a pretty damn devious item for a kid to tote around. We also made sure we had plenty of ammunition. We punched holes in a small coffee can and tied a sturdy string to it to make a shoulder pouch that could carry extra darts, point side down for safety, of course.

Our weapons factory was in Bo's basement. He had everything we needed for construction. Of course we had to perform a trial run to see if the blowgun would work. After several rounds perforated a closet door, we decided to relocate our testing range to the Master, so Bo would not become collateral damage for destroying his house. We hung a poster over the door before we left to cover any signs of vandalism.

We resumed practice once we were safely concealed in the Forest. It took several attempts before we figured out the proper circumference of the tail cone and length for the dart. The next thing to determine was the weapon's capable range and striking effectiveness. We set up a target on the tree and commenced firing. It didn't take long before we were hitting our mark. We moved back a few steps after each round.

Rhino was standing next to the Master and yelled to Skip, who was about 50 feet away. Rhino was not the sharpest knife in the drawer, not like we were all in danger of winning a Nobel Prize. Again, we were kids! He uttered these fateful words, "See if you can reach me." Skip was more than happy to oblige his request. It turned out, he could and he did.

We all watched as the dart silently left the shiny copper tube. We were able to visibly track the trajectory, as it did not possess the explosive power of a speeding bullet. It floated effortlessly through the air and dipped slightly towards the end of its flight, like a perfect breaking ball pitch, thrown by Sandy Koufax. The dart struck the bewildered youngster in the lower left shin and stuck very firmly. The target went down like a prized Caribou during a safari. The group stood in awe at this demonstration. Had the holder of the weapon allowed for proper windage and loss of velocity, the results might have been much more tragic.

Rhino lie on the ground, appropriately making sounds like a wounded animal. He instinctively popped the dart out of his leg to stop the piercing pain. I imagine it would have felt like a nail being driven into your body. I had no intention of finding out. It looked painful. Fortunately, the shin area is not known for profuse bleeding so there was only a little trickle coming from the small hole in Rhino's leg. He was more in shock that not only did the dart strike him, but he had precipitated the incident. He had requested Skip to shoot at him. There would be no retaliatory strike. The shooter and shootee immediately reconciled.

We were all impressed with this event. The topper was when Knapsack pulled a fresh bottle of Bactine and band-aids from his bag. It was about time someone had figured this out. There would have to be no awkward explanation as to why there was a hole in Rhino's shin. We ruled this weapon as overkill for our defensive mission. A misdirected shot could inflict crippling damage. We were stupid kids, not gangsters. We kept the blowguns handy at the Master for entertainment and to ward off offensive rats.

We finally devised an alternate plan to thwart an attack upon the Forest. We didn't have to wait long to put it in motion. We had hoped for the best, that Dofort would disappear into oblivion and never return. That would not be the case. He returned, and this time, with friends. We were fortunate enough to spot the group prior to them entering the Forest. There were only four of them but they were all Second-Rounders. They were bigger than us, but we had home court advantage.

We went straight to DEFCON 1 and implemented the plan. Since Bo was the fastest among us, he would act as the mechanical rabbit that the dogs would chase in the race, hopefully futilely, or Bo would have been dead meat. There were two main entrances to the Forest but we knew of others along the tree line. Bo ran directly toward the foursome and called them big ugly slobs. They took the bait and began the chase. The rest of us circled into the Forest from other angles.

Our job as kids was to run all of the time. Second-Rounders had either cut drastically back on this physical activity or had eliminated it altogether. They were no match for Bo. He had to slow down so he didn't lose them as he ran into the Kahn backyard. The Kahns' had installed a four-foot high, silver metal chain-link fence around the perimeter of their yard, which backed up to the Forest. Fortunately for us, they had also installed both front and rear, swinging gates. We had intricate working knowledge of these swinging gates. The gates would swing in both directions and lock shut when it returned to the pole position.

Bo easily cleared the first gate and left it open as an invitation to his pursuers. They followed. He slowed up once again so the group got the feeling they were closing ground on him. As he cleared the second, rear gate, they were only a couple yards behind him. He grabbed hold of the gate as he ran through the opening and swung it backwards with all his might. It immediately locked in place. The Second-Rounders never saw it coming. They ran head long into the gate causing the first two bodies to strike it with such force their bodies hung over the top of it, as the second two galoots ran into them. Phase 1 had been completed. Phase 1: Initiate the pursuit. They were now sufficiently pissed and not thinking rationally. Their prime focus was on catching and killing Bo.

The rest of us had headed directly to the Master to arm ourselves. We would then rendezvous with the rabbit at our second critical attack point. Bo now had some very angry dudes in pursuit. He had to be careful as one slip or trip would result in disaster for him. Bo headed for the Bamboo Jungle. Remember that this was a maze of our own design and construction. We all had been in it hundreds of times, enough to run it blindfolded. The Second-Rounders followed.

Bo quickly cut into the tall grass and immediately disappeared. He was able to make his way out the other side before the foursome had entered. They were lost three seconds into the maze. That would not be the worst part of the maze for them. Bo joined the rest of us on top of the adjacent hill that overlooked the Bamboo Jungle. We watched the group from our vantage point and laughed out loud as they stumbled through the crisscrossing paths into dead ends. Then we opened fire upon them from our supply of dirt bombs we had carefully stored in an old metal pail for just such the occasion. Phase 2: Instill panic.

We waited at a distance for them to finally emerge, a little worse for wear. We made sure they saw us as they came out. We weren't done with them yet and we had to lead them away from the Master and our lair. They followed obediently. We knew exactly where to duck and weave around the painful sticker bushes that rip you face along the trail. We had been introduced to them on several occasions. The pursuers were unfamiliar with this hazard. We could hear them yelling as they tried to run after us. We also knew where the holes were. They did not. Every few minutes we could hear a thud and almost hear the whoosing of air being expelled from a body as it hit the ground. Phase 3: Inflict damage and question their purpose. They definitely had questions.

We zigzagged around trees like we had never zigzagged before. We gave them a good run for their money. We headed to the Forest Butt. We easily cleared the ditch as we had done countless times before. We waited on the other side for our victims. The hunters had become the hunted. They ran up to the ditch not understanding that they needed a full run to get across it in one leap. They did not understand why we were standing on the other side looking back at them. They climbed down into the ditch to come after us. The dampness of the dirt walls slowed their progress and caused them to continually slide back in. We turned away from them and ran a few yards. To our corralled guests it looked like we were running away until we turned back towards them. We ran straight at them and then over them. We cleared their heads by a good two feet. They had no time to comprehend what was happening or think to reach up and grab us as we flew over. Phase 4: Steal their hope.

We ran a short distance and took up our positions once again. We watched as all four mud covered rascals climb out of the Crack. They spotted us as if it were their idea. This was their last charge and they came hard. They closed the distance between us in record time. They figured they would have us as soon as they crossed this open space of "dry grass." The same dry grass that housed hundreds of really pissed off Yellow Jackets. This time we had carefully circumvented the grass area and stood at the opposite side of the patch. It had appeared to the big guys that we had taken a direct route across the grass. We were lucky that the attack on our Forest had come while the weather was still hot and the wasps were very active. They were about to get a lot more active in about 10 seconds. We wanted no part of this action and high tailed it out of there to watch from a safe distance.

Dofort and his companions met with the same fate that we had suffered. The swarm arose from their underground nests with the fury of nature scorned. When we had wandered into their homes unexpectedly, we were meandering. These big oafs had come charging in like a herd of wild bulls. They were about to pay dearly for their rudeness. They immediately began the same dance we had performed, swatting and spinning wildly. We watched from the safety of the peanut gallery. We were laughing, but we had compassion. We all yelled at once, "Run!" They followed our instructions and the three of them took off yelling and jumping and swatting.

Wait. There had been four trespassers that had chased Bo through the Forest. In all the excitement of yelling and jumping and swatting, we had somehow lost track of the fourth intruder. The Gun involuntarily lurched forward from the group, falling to the ground. Ray Black, the missing piece of the puzzle, had come up behind us and shoved Gun in the back with all of his might.

Black had had difficulty climbing out of the Forest Butt due to the moist mud walls, as his buddies were already charging at us and about to enter the Wasps' nesting area. Just as Black inched his body over the top of the crack he witnessed his friends performing some type of tribal dance within a small clearing up ahead. He must have thought, why weren't they completing the attack? When Black moved closer towards the unexplained dance, he figured out that something was amiss. He paused at a distance and concealed himself behind a tree, out of view from the rest of the Knights. He watched helplessly at the yelling and the jumping and the swatting. He could do nothing to help his friends but watch.

Ray Black was about three years older than us. He was a true Second-Rounder and a scourge to our existence. He was the designated annoying bully of the Bowl (DABB). The worst part about Black was that his house sat directly across from Tommy Gun. Black never missed an opportunity to mess with our group, especially the Gun. This was probably the reason Black had singled out Gun from the rest of us as we stood watching the others flee the Forest.

This time Ray Black had committed the fatal bully error. He relied on his aggressive move to scare off the rest of us. He assumed we would run for our lives after seeing Gun hurled to the ground. And yes, the old adage was partially correct on this occasion. By assuming, Black had made an ass of himself but not the rest of us. Ray Black had no intention of fighting because bullies don't fight, they coerce. His option of not fighting was removed from the table.

Gun slowly rose to his feet as the rest of us encircled Black. Ray Black stood there trying to be all, full of himself for scoring a, cheap shot, hit upon Gun. Black understood he was bigger than each of us but he was not bigger than all of us. If we had chosen, we could have easily jumped him and beat him into the ground. We did not choose to do so. None of us had ever been involved in a real fight before. We were the best at fake fights, but in those reenactments, no physical punches were ever landed. This one would be the real deal. We did not jump Black for two reasons. One was that we were chicken shits and two, it appeared as if Black had specifically challenged Gun to a duel of fisticuffs, unintentionally or not. It was going to be Riff versus Bernardo and this time no knives.

Gun took up his position to engage his longtime nemesis. This was surely no Clay-Liston boxing match by any means. The only comparison to be drawn was that Gun was the younger, more agile fighter, against an older and uglier foe. Black threw the first flurry of punches out of sheer self-preservation. It wasn't until Black connected with the left side of Gun's jaw did the light go on for Gun. Gun paid little attention to the slight trickle of blood coming from his mouth. He sailed into the larger boy with all his pent up anger and paid back all the past abuse in spades. Black went down. We couldn't believe our eyes as we all instantly time traveled to the Clay (now Ali) / Liston rematch, where the young brass fighter stood over his beaten opponent, telling him to get up. Gun instructed him, "We're done here, now get out of our Forest." Gun had sucked all of the bully out of Black's ego. From this day forward, Ray would be known as the Black Hole, because the bullying energy could no longer escape from his body. He would never intimidate anyone again.

Black got up and sheepishly walked to his friends that stood outside the Forest line. They never looked back and they never returned. They were given a clear message that this was our Forest. We didn't need weapons. The Forest was our greatest ally and Gun was our true secret weapon. Phase 5: Conquer!

We feared that we might suffer delayed retribution by the defeated First-Rounders. We soon came to realize that they would not take any action against us. They knew if they did, the word would get out that they were bested by a bunch of little shits. What happens in the Forest, stays in the Forest.

CHAPTER TWENTY-FIVE

THE LOUISIANA PURCHASE

This chapter has absolutely nothing to do with any land purchase from France. It is my way of telling you that we continued our exploration and added a great deal of property to our Forest. Although the great purchase of the entire center of the United States was a bargain, our acquisition didn't cost us a dime so France can suck it. You can only sit in an underground lair for so long before you get the need to move on. Ask any famous evildoer; it's all about world conquest. However, we were not looking for dominance outside of the Forest. The maintenance aspect would have been way too much work. We continued on.

Heading northeast from the grass island that we almost incinerated, was a large flat field that ran along side the northbound lane of the Parkway. The State provided a buffer area of about 100 feet from where the developer would build 200 single-family homes. They also planted a few trees off the roadway to prevent the errant vehicle from landing in someone's backyard barbeque. This did nothing to deaden the constant hum of passing traffic, but the new homeowners didn't give it a second thought when it came time to sign their lives away at the closing of the purchase. Newer roadways would eventually have monolithic concrete walls erected to protect nearby residents from offending vehicular sound.

We found our new playing field. We still had to use the chronically crooked field next to Knapsack's house for baseball. Any foul ball hit at this new field would cause a major traffic pileup, for which we did not want to take responsibility. The new land would be our football field, as close to regulation size as we were going to get. We already had the plateau behind the Castle, but that space was more like a high desert with scroungey weeds and a lot of rocks.

This field was State property and part of the right-of-way of the Parkway, and was well maintained. It was rock free, complete with nice green grass that was mowed on a regular schedule. This playing field came at no cost to us well, maybe to our parents, who were paying for it in what would become the highest property taxes in the country, but we didn't concern ourselves with the minor details. We claimed it as our own.

This new space allowed us to move our semi-touch football game out of the street and far away from the Bud-mobile, no-go territory. Skip was grateful for this venue relocation as he almost experienced a gender change during a collision with a stubborn fire hydrant. He was clearly out of bounds as he stepped on the curb to make a catch. He hit the yellow metal midget on a full run. His body folded over the little guy and he spun around on the top of the octagon bolt cap for a few revolutions as if he were a compass needle trying to find true north. His limp body poured off the hydrant onto the dog-scented ground. That was another game called on account of crying. This new space permitted the almost-touch football game to become full contact tackle football. We saw no need for the addition of any type of personal protective equipment including cups or helmets.

We would mark boundaries with whatever was at hand; hats, bags, garbage, or other clothing. We were fortunate to have a football available for most games. When that was not the case we would roll up a shirt. This eliminated any spiral throws and a kickoff was no longer an option. We made do with whatever was available to us and it worked fine. When we had an odd number of players, the best quarterback played for both sides without a center. There was also a no tackling the QB rule, so he had a lot of time. This allowed everyone else to be receivers or defenders. As you can imagine, a play ran ten times longer than the typical NFL four second down. Guys would run in circles until someone managed to get free. There were no parked cars to depend upon for protection or fire hydrants to create numbing pain.

Football games developed similar to our pickup baseball games. There was never a schedule or a plan. They happened spontaneously. We headed directly to the field whenever there were enough kids around. We allowed non-Knights to participate as this field was located outside the Forest. All ages were welcome to increase the chances of enough people to field two teams. The age range was limited with football due to the full contact aspect. If need be, an ambulance could have driven directly onto the field to pick up any collateral damage. We always looked at the bright side of disasters. Surprisingly, the only serious injury turned out to be a walk off. Tommy Gun dove for a fumble and another player decided to stupidly soccer-kick the ball away. Unfortunately for the Gun, the kid connected with his nose instead, making a loud sound that even the non-medically- trained person could detect as a break. It was similar to the much later, Lawrence Taylor/

Joe Theismann collision, but not as disgustingly loud. We did not call the game this time because Gun was the biggest and strongest out of the eight of us. He was our gentle giant, good thing for us. The Gun walked home bloody but not beaten (I still retained the title for the most blood after the swinging chair incident).

Knapsack came through with a handy towel from his bag for Gun to wrap his face. It would have been perfect if he had pulled a bag of frozen peas from his bag but that was not the case. Still, he was getting better at this preparation thing. Gun returned a few days later, after a mother-induced time out period, with a slightly bent nose. It gave him character, not that he needed any more.

To the south of the grass island were two manmade items that piqued our interest. The first was a large storm water pipe, even larger than the one they had buried in our street. This pipe made it possible to move the water off the six-lane roadway above, and prevented vehicles from hydroplaning as they crossed the non-descript bridge (over the river). The pipe had a perpetual flow of water running along the bottom, a couple of inches deep. We could easily walk inside by ducking down and straddling the water to keep our feet to dry. There was a straight run back into the pipe for about 50 yards before it angled to the left and right into a T connection. There was an eerie light that shone down from a grate positioned directly above the T. The grate allowed in enough light so the pipe was not a black hole. The challenge was to see how far we could go into the sewer pipe before we turned back.

We immediately dubbed our new find, The Drain. The first several steps into the Drain were a piece of cake. After twenty or so steps, my feet became noticeably heavier and my body moved at half speed. My mind was racing with thoughts of the "Flush." I imagined a humongous hand pressing down on a similarly large lever. This action would trigger the expected result of a million gallons of disgusting toilet water emptying from the Bowl, headed in my direction. There would be a tremendous sound of rushing water as if the entire ocean was being funneled into this drain directly at me. Before I could turn my body to flee towards the freedom that lie out in the safety of the sunlight, this wall of putrid, maggot gagging sludge would engulf and overpower me, sweeping my scrawny kid body out into the river, never to be seen again. I would have become just another forgotten turd, on its way to obscurity. Needless to say, I never made it to the T intersection.

Some of the other Knights invented their own horror story of death. The Mechanic saw in his mind, an angry pack of giant, lice-infested, rats waiting to tear the flesh from his bones. Although our death scenarios were highly improbable, they could not be totally ruled out as impossible, so in essence, they could happen. Bo was the only one of us that was either stupid enough or brave enough to not only reach the T, but also make the turn. Most made it into the pipe about 25 feet before fleeing for their lives. We finally decided to bypass this endeavor for saner pursuits and eliminate these nightmares.

By saner, I mean different. We really had no clear definition of the word sane. We traveled a bit further past the drain until we reached the river. The six-lane Parkway overpass was at this location. The bridge was held up at the center by a massive concrete center support that ran perpendicular to the road. To build this structure, the engineers designed a man-made island in the center of the river to anchor the support structure. Over time, the river deposited sediment around the construction to form a real dirt island around the concrete.

We were able to jump onto the center island from the bank because the river was very narrow on our side of the river, with the major water flow being directed around the far side at no man's land. This led us to the center of the bridge, actually two separate bridges, each holding one direction of traffic above us. The concrete wall was four feet wide and at least ten feet high where the steel beams rested, supporting the road above that. The wall ran the entire width of both roadways with a gap in the middle, as if they put a giant window in the bridge.

For the same reason we tried to cross the river, we needed to climb this wall at the gap, because it was there. This was a plain concrete wall with no handgrips or foot holds to be found. This did not deter us, as we possessed kid ingenuity and persistence, plus we had a lot of time on our hands. We climbed each other, with the base guy leaning against the wall, enabling us to reach the flat surface at the top of the wall. We were in the middle of the parkway, but well below and out of sight of passing motorists.

It took several attempts before we reached the correct formula on who would be the first one, and who would be last one, up the wall. The smallest guy would be easy to lift to the top first, but he wasn't strong enough to grab a heavier guy. We settled on lifting the biggest guy present in the middle of the order, so there was enough power to lift him, and then an equal power remaining to assist him to the top. Once one guy was settled, he was able to grab the next one from above. We continued the procedure until there was one of us left. The last guy would take a short run, on the limited island, and literally run up the wall to be caught in mid flight by the rest of us, and hoisted up. Marines would have envied our ability at adapting and overcoming this obstacle.

To dismount was a lot easier. We would cinch our bodies over the side and then lower ourselves until we were only holding on by our hands. We would then kick back off the wall and jump down onto the dirt. Leaving the wall always made me think of my mother's mantra. She said this phrase to me hundreds of times, "If your friends jumped off a bridge; would you?" I guess the answer was yes.

There wasn't much to do sitting on top of a concrete wall as cars whizzed by us, usually traveling faster than the posted speed limit. The most we could manage was to listen to some music from someone's small transistor radio or eat a snack from home. We also engaged in imaginary match up battles. What if Superman fought Frankenstein? Given enough time, we could have solved all of mankind's problems. We never gave a thought that we had exceeded the boundaries of our Forest. If Dorothy had abandoned her deadly profile of killing witches and decided to eliminate little boys, or the Tree Man returned for a more, sporty hunt, no one would think to look under the bridge for our bodies.

We continued to journey into space in 1965. This became a very costly hobby because NASA believed crashing into the moon with Ranger 8 was considered a successful mission. The spacecraft had photographed possible landing sites for our future astronauts that Kennedy had promised. I found it odd that NASA did not see a need to turn a multi-million dollar piece of equipment around to be used again. My guess was they reasoned we could make more cameras. This was truly one of the most expensive disposable cameras ever made.

In March, 3,500 Marines arrive in Da Nang, South Vietnam to assist all the advisors that had previous been sent there to "advise." This action was recognized as bringing the first of America's combat troops in the country. Back home, protestors against the war were burning their draft cards. To a few, the biggest outrage was when Bob Dylan went electric. Martin Luther King Jr. was deploying his own troops as 25,000 marched from Selma, Alabama to Montgomery.

On September 9th, LA Dodger, Sandy Koufax, pitched a perfect game against the Chicago Cubs. A "no hitter" is a misnomer. It doesn't mean no one hit the ball. It means no one on the Cubs reached first base on a hit. The Knights could clearly empathize with the losing team that day as none of us had yet reached first base. We were eleven years old, so our hormones had not yet been redirected to our next sole purpose in life. We knew about first base. Some of us may have started to dream about second base. Third base may have been located on Mars as far as we knew and a home run existed in another dimension.

CHAPTER TWENTY-SIX

THE HANGMAN'S NOOSE

W e thought riding bicycles was the best thing in the world. That was, until the gasoline engine came into our lives. Two of the Knights, Bo and the Mechanic, were fortunate enough to acquire kid-size motorcycles. They were called mini bikes. They were small, motorized vehicles. They were built low to the ground and had tires much wider than a bicycle. They operated the same as a motorcycle with a hand throttle to provide the engine with gas but no gears. The problem with these machines was that they were not legal to operate on the street. We were not yet old enough to acquire a valid license even if the mini bikes were street legal. The bikes were also not built for off-road as dirt bike motorcycles used in Motocross racing.

So where do you operate these bikes? The answer was, pretty much anywhere you can get away with operating them, which included on the street and in the Forest. This drew unwanted attention from killjoy neighbors that were offended by the whiney sound that they made. This was ironic as they lived between two major roadways that were never quiet. They would often call the local police to chase us away. I'm sure the officers were ecstatic when they received the big call over their patrol car radio. It was always a lose-lose event. The police were called and broke no speed records arriving. Usually the angry neighbor would unwillingly warn us by yelling out their front door, "I called the cops on you damn kids!" This provided ample time for the riders to get home and secure their machines in their garages.

The police surprised us on one occasion when they actually got their cop butts out of their patrol car and walked up to the Forest. They met us as the bunch of us was walking out into the Weiner yard. The one officer said to us, "Do you guys have any mini bikes?" My stupid reflex instinctively kicked in and I patted my pockets and replied, "Nope, I don't have any". I knew I was dead as the words left my mouth. The cop walked over to me and breathed his cop breath all over me, as he duly noted, "What are you, a smart-ass?" It was clearly a rhetorical question as I certainly was a smart-ass as demonstrated by my ass talking back to him, however not very intelligently. No other words needed to be exchanged and so the nice officers returned to, their real patrol duties and fighting crime. We were all clear on the message that had been delivered. Do not make a non-situation into something that could remove your television viewing into the next century. Had the cop punched me in my smart-ass mouth, which I totally deserved, there would be no retelling this incident to my parents, whereupon I may have received a second blow for good measure.

Bo and the Mechanic were not thrilled that I had upped the ante for the police actually catching one of them riding their offending bikes. They now had to be more cautious during their rides. They were extremely careful not to ride in traffic and they never tore up any of the neighbors' properties. On the few occasions they took their bikes into the Forest, they remained on the outskirts, in the grassy perimeter, so they wouldn't tear up their machines on the dirt and rocky paths. They were magnanimous enough to allow each of us to take the bikes for a ride. If we screwed around, our privileges were revoked. There would be no appeal. We learned to respect this generous offer. After all, there was also a monetary cost involved for operation and repairs. Liability was never a concern. The general population was not yet consumed with suing each other for the slightest incident. When I was 9 years old, my sister's friend broke my arm. I don't think I even received a get-well card.

The Mechanic and Bo were always careful. They never met Murphy but if they did, they would learn he was one son of a bitch. He was famous for saying, "If something can go wrong, it will". On that one day when nothing was going wrong, Bo was motoring about on his nice shiny blue mini bike. The same safety rules applied to riding a motorized bike as applied to playing on playground equipment. That would be, none. We never wore helmets riding our regular bikes. Why would we? The same thought process carried over to riding a faster bike. Why bother. That also applied to eye protection. The first we ever heard about real safety rules was from our nine-fingered shop class teacher. He had gone that extra mile to make a point about safety. He was very good. On this day, a helmet would not have saved Bo.

Bo had chosen to ride on the sidewalk as his preferred course. He may have been out for a joy ride or headed to one of our houses. He never reached his destination. There was a tree service working in the neighborhood at this time. They had already cut down the major portion of a large tree and were preparing to remove the trunk. Unlike the Knights, they followed safety regulations because this was dangerous work. They properly roped off the tree to control the angle and location that the trunk would fall. They were concentrating on their job. They did not see the young boy approaching on his nice shiny blue mini bike.

As they say, timing is everything. As Bo entered the work zone, the rope lay limp across the sidewalk. At the exact moment Bo approached the rope, the tree crew pulled hard on it to remove the slack to the tree before they toppled it. The rope jumped up in front of Bo, probably before he ever saw it. The heavy thick rope caught Bo evenly across his throat. The now taunt rope held strong. Bo's 100 lb. body was no match for the object. It flung him upwards and backwards off the seat of his mini bike. The tree crew saw the aftermath of the impact as Bo's body was flung to the ground. The bike continued out of control for a few more yards until it spun to the ground.

The tree crew ran to his aid hoping the boy wasn't dead. Bo had experienced a super Hemowasi, was thrown off a moving motorbike at about 10 mph, landed backwards on a concrete sidewalk (without a helmet), and lived to tell about it. The best thing was that he walked away with visible proof of this tale. The coarse rope had only contacted Bo's skin for a matter of seconds but had burned a very conspicuous hangman's mark across the front of his throat. If you are a kid, there is absolutely nothing cooler than a scar like this. Thankfully for Bo, it faded in time, but it was nonetheless cool as hell while it lasted. Bo achieved legend status up there with the Tree Man. In a way, this also made him a tree man of sorts. He was proud to open his button down shirt and show off the mark to anyone who asked to see it. The girls of course thought it was gross. Bo's parents disposed of the wretched machine as quickly as possible.

1966 was all about popularity. President Johnson stated that America should stay in Vietnam until the Communist threat was ended. He brought the troop strength in that country up to 190,000. By year's end it was up to a quarter of a million. This did not make him a popular guy, because the Vietnam War was not popular by any means. The Beatles announced that they were more popular than Jesus. This may or may not have been true, seeing that Jesus was not on the pop charts and the Beatles were. By saying it was true, the Beatles became less popular.

Bobbi Gibb was the first woman to compete in the Boston Marathon. This event was probably only popular with women at that time. Charles Whitman started a new unpopular and infamous trend by killing random people at the University of Texas at Austin. This was possibly the only incident that everyone agreed was to be a very bad and tragic thing, besides the death of Walt Disney. Walt Disney had created the happiest place on Earth. The world was quickly running out of happy places.

CHAPTER TWENTY-SEVEN

THE HAUNTED HOUSE

We always continued exploring, whether we were in the Forest or outside of it. Sometimes we would take another route home from school that started at the back of the Castle. There were three land tiers going south. The Castle sat on the top tier. The next tier was down a sharp hill of about 50 feet that led to an open flat field. The field area measured approximately 300 x 300 yards. It was larger than the actual school property above it. The Knights had previously eliminated this space for football because the grass next to the Parkway was so much better. Both locations were equidistant from the center of the Bowl but in our minds, the Parkway was closer. The school would totally underutilize this space and left it for us to play softball or kickball. If they had sunk some money into the damn place, it could have been awesome.

We ventured to the far edge of this plateau as if it were the edge of Christopher Columbus' flat world. There was another fifty-foot drop that overlooked Route 22. Between the top of the second tier and the highway stood the house. It was a very old-looking abandoned structure. It was clear that it was haunted. If you looked up the definition of haunted house in the dictionary you would see a picture of this house.

What is the first thing you do when you find a haunted house? You throw crap at it. So we threw rocks at the house to make sure it was unoccupied. I'm not positive this is an accepted scientific principle but it worked for us. The house did not respond to our inquiry. Most of the windows had already been broken out so we finished the job. This was not a simple task considering the size of the glass panes, the distance from the summit, and the angle at which we were launching our projectiles. The major handicap was that we had lousy hand-eye coordination. In some circles, breaking windows of a property that is not your own is considered vandalism. We didn't know the meaning of the word vandalism. We didn't know the meaning of a lot of words. We rationalized it wasn't bad because the house was already dead. You can't hurt a dead thing.

Eventually we moved closer. We eased down the hill, just in case the house could hear us. We approached one of the doors that stood hanging open. It was calling for us to enter. We had flashbacks of the drain filled with hordes of rats and the giant flush that would carry us away. It was the same unknown danger that awaited us in a different terrifying form. Another test. We were a year older than when we did or did not enter the drain. You would think we were a year smarter. Nah. There were no stairs leading to the broken door. We had to physically climb on the remnants of the missing cinder block stairway to get inside.

We pushed and hoisted each other until we could stand inside the doorway. We were standing in a narrow dark hallway. Skip was lucky enough to find himself as the lead person of our expedition. He had no way of relinquishing his leadership position as it was bestowed upon him by the full confidence of the group. In other words he was the first person that climbed inside. Forward was the only direction left for Skip to go! He moved slowly down the hallway.

He had only managed a few steps before his right foot disappeared through the rotted wooden floor. Hoops had been standing directly behind Skip and quickly grabbed him back before Skip's momentum propelled his entire body into the basement. There was, of course, no electrical power to the house but a light bulb finally went on in our collective heads. We took a silent vote and backed out of the house. Once outside we unanimously decided to only use the house as target practice. It wasn't worth the risk for further exploration of the interior. Surprisingly, Bo agreed. I assumed that had been a substantially hard yank off the mini bike by the hangman. It may have knocked some sense into the little guy.

The winter brought us a new sport. We had snowballs to launch at the house. We now had to trek across the now frozen field that had transformed into tundra like conditions, to reach the edge of the plateau. Throwing snowballs at an inanimate object kept us amused for a long time, like a cat with a ball of yarn. The challenge eventually diminished and we sought out a more challenging target. The answer was staring right at us. The highway sat directly in front of us, beyond the house. There was an endless supply of potential targets passing us by.

The concept of hitting a moving car from this distance was at most, abstract. We figured it would pass the time by trying. We were at least fifty feet above the highway and another seventy-five feet away from it. We began our wintry barrage with absolutely no luck. Hoops possessed the best arm in the group so was soon closing in on hitting the sidewalk of the roadway in front of the house. It's true that practice makes perfect and we were all soon catching up to Hoops.

It took a great deal of skill to not only to clear the distance from the edge of the hill down to the highway, but also to time the movement of a vehicle traveling at fifty miles an hour to perfectly intercept it with a porous snowball. The trick was to throw the snowball straight out as soon as a car or truck cleared the trees down below to our left. The closest lane brought the vehicles from left to right into our line of sight. We were getting the knack of this. In time we were landing sporadic hits on random targets.

We were totally absorbed in our target practice. We didn't notice the brake lights come on one car after a fairly good strike. Our concentration was on the rest of vehicles below passing by. We were not looking back towards the tundra. We didn't expect the driver to pull off at the next exit into the Bowl. We never figured a person would be so totally pissed to park his car and climb the other side of the hill from the neighborhood to the plateau. We never thought someone would cross the snow-covered field seeking the source of snowballs that had rained down upon his car.

The stranger came up from behind us, scaring the hell out of us, as the Tree Man had done in the Forest. He was upon us before we had a chance to react, which in this case meant run. Fortunately, this person was not carrying a weapon. This was our first encounter with a new, sometimes contact sport called road rage. It wasn't pretty. He calmed down a bit after seeing that we were just a bunch of morons and not older assholes. We stood in silence as he rightfully berated us, literally spitting out his words in cold puffs of frost. When he was through with his rant, he turned, red faced, and stomped off through the snow to return to his car. He felt better and we felt terrible.

We stood there like little kids that had shit their pants. We were speechless for maybe the first time in our lives. The irate stranger was totally right. We didn't hear all the words he was yelling at us but we retained the gist of it. This activity was stupid and disrespectful of others. The phrase that really stuck with us was that it was dangerous. After all, we were The Knights of the Forest and these actions went against the entire Code of Chivalry. We had never thought about the consequences of striking a car going fifty miles an hour, that the impact could possibly break the windshield or distract the driver significantly enough to swerve out of control and become involved in a serious collision.

A total stranger had schooled us properly. We left our sniper's nest for the last time. There was no point in returning to this location. This had been a good lesson that we learned before there had been any tragic consequences. We were also thankful to have lived through another unfriendly encounter.

CHAPTER TWENTY-EIGHT

GROOVIN'

It was unusually muggy that July day. Tiny water droplets hung over the river, creating a soft mist. We all knew this was an extraterrestrial phenomenon that was responsible for this eerie environment. It felt more like the dead of August, when the heat would be oppressive, making you sweat bullets just standing still. It was too hot for football at the Parkway clearing or basketball at Rhino's backyard court. No one felt like standing in the sun for baseball. There was only the eight of us anyway and not enough players to field two teams. It was kind of a do nothing day so we decided we would hang out in the Forest, where it was slightly cooler under the shade of the trees.

We greeted Gray Rock as our routine, all touching it as we passed it. Our unspoken telepathic destination was The Master. The majority of the gang climbed aboard and nestled into their favorite niche among the boughs. Knapsack and Bo decided to hang out on the ground. Knapsack rummaged thru his bag and pulled out a small transistor radio to break up the monotony. Quickly tuning it in to basically the only radio station that could be picked up in the Forest, he turned up the sound from 77 WABC, being broadcasted live from New York City. It was appropriate that the Young Rascals' hit, "Groovin'," was playing because it was a Sunday afternoon and we were certainly groovin'.

> Groovin' on a Sunday afternoon
> Really couldn't get away too soon
> I can't imagine anything that's better
> The world is ours whenever we're together
> There ain't a place I'd like to be instead of
> Movin' down a crowded avenue

Bo must have gotten a sudden burst of energy as his schooch gene kicked in. He grabbed Knapsack's bag and engaged him in a game of keep-a-way. This was yet another means of torture we all enjoyed, unless the object being kept away belonged to us. The rest of us cheered on both guys from our perch, Knapsack being the unwilling party to these shenanigans. Bo, the smallest of the group, was the most agile. He was able to duck and run as he outmaneuvered his desperate opponent. Bo soon used up all the available room below the tree and took off on a sprint. Knapsack was no slouch and was in hot pursuit directly behind his prey. We all leaped from the tree, not willing to miss any of the action.

We immediately forgot about the heat and how lazy we had been minutes prior to the chase. The music faded as we ran further from the tree.

> Doing anything we like to do
> There's always lots of things that we can see
> You can be anyone we like to be
> All those happy people we could meet
> Just groovin' on a Sunday afternoon
> Really, couldn't get away too soon

No, No, No...

Bo was on a mad dash to escape capture. He could hear the rest of us yelling far behind him and Knapsack. The procession weaved in out of trees and over small bushes. Eventually we reached the Bamboo Jungle with everyone disappearing inside of it. There was a great deal of rustling in the tall grass. The small animals of the Forest were probably thinking a wild congress of baboons were on a stampede. Squirrels and rabbits were quick to get out of this rolling path of destruction.

We'll keep on spending sunny days this way
We're gonna talk and laugh our time away
I feel it coming closer day by day
Life would be ecstasy, you and me endlessly

Bo emerged at the other end of the Jungle, which left him only one escape route. The hill lay directly in front of him. If he could navigate the narrow gravel path he could double back and disappear into the Forest. Knapsack burst out of the weeds just in time to see the scrawny kid begin his ascent. This was definitely a race for King of the Hill. Bo had a good lead as Knapsack huffed up the stones behind him. When Knapsack looked up to check his closing distance, Bo was gone. He thought there was no way Bo could have cleared the entire hill in those few seconds.

We all heard the yell at the same time. Bo had also been checking his progress and turned to look back at Knapsack. That microsecond glance caused him to miss a critical step and his foot landed on the wrong side of the hill. His balance was totally compromised and pitched his body to the right. His speed and agility could not save him from this fateful move that prevented him from recovering. The gravel was loose and somewhat moist today, creating a slipperier than usual surface. Bo was out of control as he went, ass over teakettle, down the side of the hill.

The rest of us reached the top, where Knapsack stood in bewilderment. This was the most hysterical thing we had seen, until, until we saw Bo's body launch into the river. On most days after a slide, we were able to stand right up and shake off the spill. This was not the case on this muggy Sunday. The river appeared to be running a bit quicker and slightly higher than normal. Bo bobbed up from the water so we knew he was all right. He still wasn't getting out of the river.

We had seen a lot of changes in the Forest. We experienced all the crazy Jersey seasons and witnessed a couple wicked storms. We had not come across something known as a flash flood. This is when rapid flooding occurs to low lying areas due to severe thunderstorms. It wasn't raining today. That is, it wasn't raining where we were. Unbeknownst to us, heavy rain had been falling upstream. Besides the rain, all the runoff from all the surrounding area was pouring into the river. Over time, the area upstream had undergone a great deal of development or overdevelopment, depending upon your viewpoint. Much of the open space had been built upon and paved over. There was little area for water to be absorbed back into the ground so it flowed off of the paved surfaces. We had no idea that this tremendous volume of accumulated water had been heading our way as we lounged in the tree.

Bo started to move downstream. What was worse was that he had placed the arm straps from the knapsack over his shoulders so it would provide more mobility during his escape. The bag was acting as a float that was carrying him away. He was too busy trying to keep his head above water to slip the bag off his body. On the positive side it was maintaining his buoyancy. This was a double-edged sword.

We were all yelling as we ran down Bo's original escape route to the Forest. We could see the water level and flow increasing before our eyes. The bank was too high off the river in most parts for us to try and reach out for him. All we could do was try and keep up with his movement. This wasn't easy because we had to run around objects while he pretty much has a straight shot downstream. We were thankful for the few rocks and tree limbs that protruded above the surface that helped slow him down. Bo was still unable to latch onto any of these objects as he bounced off them like a silver ball in a pinball game. One by one these objects disappeared below the surface as the water rose.

We all heard the sound at once. It was someone blowing a whistle. Bo had managed to grasp the whistle that Knapsack at attached to the outside of his bag with a lanyard. Bo continued to blow the whistle while trying to keep his head above water. This enabled us to track his whereabouts as we ran parallel with the river.

We all knew the Forest and we knew the river. We also knew that we only had one chance to save our friend. If he passed the highway bridge to the south he was a goner. There would be no way we would be able to get to him. The problem was that our only shot was at the beach. The beach was directly before the bridge. We were all screaming out the plan as we ran like we had never run before. Bo was frantically blowing the whistle.

It was a miracle but we had reached the beach prior to Bo's arrival. We jumped down onto the beach, which was now under water. It was only up to our calves but at least it was a level surface where we could still execute our rescue. The plan was simple. Grab Bo as he went by. The hard part was that we had to reach him. The beach did not go out far enough. We made a human chain holding onto each other, almost tying ourselves together with what little clothing we could grasp. Gun was the hook because he was the strongest and it would take a maximum effort to grab Bo from the clutches of the river. Skip was the anchor holding onto a tree at the bank. The rest of us formed the rest of the links in the chain. Every one of us was vital to the rescue plan.

We waded out farther into the river to block Bo's path and intercept him. We didn't anticipate the force of an angry river. It was nothing any of us had experienced before. At first I thought we would all be swept away as we struggled against the powerfully increasing current. We finally found our footing and held fast. Bo was coming at us and way faster than we expected. We only had one shot at grabbing him. Skip was straining to hold onto the tree with six other bodies pulling away from him. The bark was cutting into his hands. We were all yelling for Bo to paddle closer to our side of the river. He was still struggling to get the bag off his shoulders. The water was passing our knees.

One hundred feet became fifty, then twenty feet, ten feet. Gun reached out to grab Bo and just missed Bo's arm. If Bo had slipped off Knapsack's bag it would have been all over for him. Gun was able to grab a strap from the bag and pull Bo into his body. All we had to do was to slowly make it back to the bank and we were home free. Skip's grip gave out with the extra, added weight of another body, and corresponding increase in the pull of the river. Skip let out two screams. The first was an "oh shit" scream, because he was being pulled into the river with his buddies. The second was because something had grabbed him and scared the crap out of him. At first, visions of the Tree Man went through his mind.

Not Dofort. Skip imagined that the actual legend that we had created had come to life and grabbed a hold of him.

Skip was too busy holding onto the next link in the chain to worry about what had a hold of him. He was thankful it was pulling him back up the bank. Once he had his arm around the tree again, the figure passed him and headed into the water. One by one the figure pulled us in until he reached Bo. He scooped up Bo who was now totally exhausted and carried him to higher ground. We stood around the figure as he knelt over Bo and checked him over. It was The Bud.

The Bud had been out in his yard that abutted the Forest and heard us yelling as we paralleled Bo's death-defying journey down the river. The Bud was accustomed to our average kid noise and antics. He knew immediately on this day that this was not kids' fun yelling. After determining that Bo was breathing all right, The Bud again picked him up and walked out of the Forest, with us following him, like half drowned ducklings following their mother.

The Bud walked directly to his 1960 mid-night blue, Cadillac Coupe Deville, with a pristine white interior and opened the door. All eight mud and river-slime covered bodies piled into both the front and back seats. He then drove us to the emergency room to get checked out. The ride was pretty quiet, mostly because we were totally spent from this exhausting adventure, but also because we couldn't believe The Bud let our disgusting bodies not only touch his once pristine white interior, but also violate it in this most vile way. The downpour that had flooded the river and stolen Bo had finally caught up to us as we sat silently in the car and watched the wipers rhythmically push the water out of the way.

We all called home, one by one, on the waiting room pay phone. The Bud also supplied the change for the call. Calling your parents from the local emergency room to get a ride home is not a call you ever want to make. It is one step up from calling from a police station, but still bad. We were hoping that The Bud would take us home and call it a day but hospitals are funny about releasing juveniles without obtaining a parent or guardian's signature. I'm also sure The Bud had had enough of us in his car. As the parents arrived, there were a lot of thank yous, hugging, kissing, and crying. When we got home there was a lot of yelling, pointing, and grounding. This was certainly to be expected and came as no surprise to the drowned rat pack.

Bo was fine but they kept him overnight for observation. Everyone, including the Bud, was given a tetanus shot for good measure, for possible exposure to harmful bacteria. The next day we waited out in front of Bo's house for his triumphant return. The first rule set down by the overjoyed and absolutely livid parents was, do not go into the woods! As soon as Bo arrived home, we all headed to the Forest. Really, you didn't expect anything less did you?

CHAPTER TWENTY-NINE

ALL GOOD THINGS MUST COME TO AN END

The flash flood waters had quickly receded as fast as they had arrived but left their mark. The river was still flowing with enthusiasm but had lost most of its fury. Our underground lair was now a muddy swimming pool. The roof and most other objects were swept away. There was a moat around the master, denying access to it, and there was a pungent smell to the entire area. The river had deposited whatever bad things existed upstream, into our Forest.

It was Monday, July 17, 1967. It was already after 5 PM when we headed out as it took a bit of finagling to get out of the now overcautious watch of the still shell shocked, mothers. After all, their babies had almost drowned. We went directly to Gray Rock after we had surveyed the damage to the surrounding area. The Tree Man had been one thing, but the previous day was something out of this world.

Our time in the Forest had come to an end. We had spent hundreds of hours on various adventures together. That was time that could never be taken away from us by man or nature. We agreed we would all meet in the future but when? Gun noted the present time and date, as he was familiar with military jargon. He stated, "It is 07/17/67 at 1717 hours. If we meet in 50 years it will be 07/17/17." That seemed like a good a time as any so we made an oath. In one half century, the Knights would reconvene at this very spot. We took a knee at Gray Rock and placed our hand upon the stone. We stated the following: "We the Knights of the Forest shall meet at this rock, at this time, in 50 years." We stood up with one muddy knee and walked home to eat dinner.

The following Saturday was consumed by a lot of scrubbing and wiping small particles of mud and slime from the interior of a 1960 midnight blue Cadillac Coupe Deville with a soon-to-be again, pristine white interior. It would be another year before the Bud-mobile would be savagely attacked by the can-opener.

We couldn't do enough for The Bud. Leaves were raked up and snow was shoveled without asking. The mothers must have delivered every type of pie and cake out of their Betty Crocker cookbooks to express their undying gratitude for saving their babies.

Mother Nature may have dealt the final blow to our escapades in the Forest but we all knew deep down inside that our stay had been running short for some time. There was an underlying current that ran not within the river, but through the neighborhood itself, that was pulling us back away from the tree line. It turned out to be the most destructive force to the Knighthood. Twelve years ago over 20 ribbons appeared outside various neighborhood doors in the Bowl. The Knights were included in these joyous birth announcements but we didn't account for all of them. Half of all those ribbons were pink in color. Those pink ribbons coexisted along with us through our many years growing up and during our time at the Castle.

For years we had feigned the obligatory fear of cooties as our excuse not to associate with the girls. Sure, we talked to them and sometimes played with them, but we shrugged it off and rationalized that this was mandatory social behavior. We never mentioned it, but we knew deep down inside that these beautiful creatures were not only different, but also special. They were softer and spoke quieter than us. The light that came from their eyes was brighter. Their laughter was gentle and honest. It was 1967 and the hairstyle was longer for both boys and girls, thanks to the British invasion. The girls all wore their hair straight and down to their waist. There was a nice variety with shades of blondes, browns, blacks, and reds. If you got too close, accidently on purpose, you could tell that they even smelled better than the rest of the Knights. They didn't fart or burp words on command.

The Knights were all smitten, and I'm talking sledgehammer smitten. The dreaded scourge of the global cooties epidemic had been eradicated from the face of the earth forever (as an adult I can truthfully testify that I have not seen another case of cooties since the early 60's). We were free to openly associate with the opposite sex. This was certainly not a bad thing. It wasn't a minute too soon, either, because our bodies were undergoing changes faster than Lawrence Talbot turning into the Wolf Man. There would be a lot of pain and howling that followed these changes.

The Knighthood broke from a pack of eight into individuals that soon paired with various pink ribbons.

"Couples" would be together for a few days or weeks, break up, and then reunite to form new couples. It was usually cordial, with the sporadic meltdown crisis, which would only last for a few days. There was never any long lasting animosity. We saved the good hatred for high school. The Knights had not been banished from the neighborhood. Instead, our group doubled in size. Our new best days were spent hanging on someone's front stoop after school just shooting the breeze.

We were given one chance to prove we were true Knights and demonstrate our chivalrous qualities. We set out to do battle to defend the pink ribbons. It didn't go exactly as we had planned. One of "our" pink ribbons somehow became involved in a love triangle with an outlier, who had already been claimed by another. Words were exchanged and the next thing we are told is that the scorned, outlier pink ribbon was seeking retribution. No problem; we had this.

I set out with the Mechanic and Knapsack to confront this problem head on. We hadn't gone far down the street when an old car screeched up to us. It contained the scorned pink ribbon, along with her older brother and his driving-age buddies. They started to pile out of the vehicle like a clown car. It seemed there was no end to the number of occupants. One oversized occupant yelled out to us if we knew the whereabouts of the third side of the triangle. We all wanted to answer, " Yeah, what are you going to do about it?" Fortunately, we paused.

Our minds began to race. We understood that Chivalry Rule Number 5 was: *Thou shalt not recoil before the enemy.* Technically, these moaks were not our enemies. We didn't even know them. They classified as third party total strangers, at this moment in time. We also understood that any confrontational conversation was going to lead to a major ass-kicking, inflicted upon the wrong parties, namely us. Knapsack drew upon his memory of English class and quickly invoked the spirit of King Henry IV – he recalled that discretion is the better part of valor. Knapsack quickly responded to the crowd of seething bullies on wheels with; "We have no idea what you are talking about." They were satisfied with that answer and climbed back into the clown car and drove off on their mission of revenge. We retained what little respect we could muster based upon a technicality. We could literally live with that. We made sure the offending pink ribbon stayed out of sight for a few days until time healed all wounds. We did not speak of this moment again.

The Knights still walked to school together in the mornings. After the 3:15 bell, we would find ourselves walking ridiculously long ways home instead of taking the shortcut down the hill. We figured that a few extra minutes to see the pink ribbons home safely wasn't an unreasonable gesture. We were still Knights and Knights were chivalrous. Besides, there were no dragons to slay and no tree men to vanquish. After all, a guy's got to fill the time somehow. Fighting dragons would have been a Sunday picnic compared to the frightening event referred to as the school dance.

This social ritual to graduate to adulthood required not only the touching of the feminine species in public but also gyrating in front of your friends. It was a totally humbling experience. We survived these dances and absolutely capitalized on opportunities to perfect what moves we thought we possessed. We had none. The girls were patient and understanding. They didn't expect a lot. After all, we were only boys.

We were very fortunate to have kept our group of eight intact for the entire run of grammar school. Although the outliers were not Knights, they had still been good friends. Out of the entire group of 44, we only lost a handful of kids due to relocation. It wasn't as traumatic as death, but moving away was just as final. There was no internet or social media. The only phone was the house phone and when you moved away you lost your phone number. Parents didn't think to provide the new address to their children's friends so they could stay in touch. When they moved, they were gone.

The last and final blow to the Knights was high school. We were all excited to enter this new phase in our lives together. We gathered up in the morning as we had done hundreds of times before. The only difference was that the school was a lot farther away, on the other side of town, and it started about an hour earlier. Who thought that was a good idea? I hated getting up before dawn. I later discovered that this was preliminary training for hating to get up even earlier, for big boy work.

Our early morning routine continued unchanged throughout our freshman year; however, the end of the day was almost immediately altered. We had no idea that high school acted as a human sieve. It was as if an invisible giant prospector scooped us up in his pan and sifted us back and forth, as if we were mineral deposits washing down a stream. One by one, we fell through separate perforations in the mesh, only large enough for one of us per hole. The process retained the course particles that we had all possessed as a group, so that the finer parts passed through to form a new, individual, refined golden nugget. This process separated us to follow an uncharted path with new interests and a new corresponding group of friends.

We had diverse schedules at the end of the day, which sent us spinning off in different directions. Some joined various team sports. Others had clubs to attend. Some went directly home and others participated in civic activities. The old group no longer existed as it had since first grade. It wasn't a bad thing. It was growing up. We had all been a part of one like-minded person up until this time. It was time to be ourselves.

It was uncanny that not only were we not in each other's classes, but we almost never saw each other throughout the course of the day. That was almost an impossible mathematical probability. There seemed to be a master plan to keep us apart and it worked. If we did happen to pass each other in the hallway, we would give an acknowledging head nod, as you would to a stranger on the street, just to be polite.

We eventually developed new sets of friends to replace the old singular group. I was fortunate that The Mechanic had spun off into my new orbit and was a part of my new friends. He had dropped his nickname because he wasn't a kid any longer. He changed it back to Ant. I heard that Knapsack also dropped his nickname. Being called sack as a teenage boy had very negative connotations. New names worked better for everyone.

The summer of 1969 was a new life, unlike any summer before it. There were new friends and new places to go. Girls were also now a big part of life. I'm sure the other Knights, like myself, forgave the pink ribbons for bringing us out of the Forest. The Knighthood became a distant memory. There would be no more collecting the group, one by one, and usual horseplay on our trek to school.

In 1969 my household consisted of two adults and two children, along with the obligatory .5 dog, to conform to the United States Census Bureau regulations. We also had one family member who stopped by for a brief period around suppertime. Sometimes he would stay all day if there was a special event taking place anywhere in the world. Uncle Walt wasn't really a true family member, he just felt like one. Most people knew him as Walter Cronkite and he anchored the evening news, before the evening news became a 24-hour event. He was referred to as "The Most Trusted Man in America". For the life of me, I could not understand why he was not the President of the United States. In just three years, Nixon caused the terms "trusted" and "President" to become mutually exclusive words. There would be a stain on the highest office in the land that would last for some time to come.

Cronkite came into our living rooms and told America the news, good or bad. On most days there was no good. He reported on the progress, or the lack thereof, in Vietnam. The most disturbing part was when they provided the number of Americans killed over a period of the previous week. The number of dead was often in the triple digits. I don't want to believe the news agencies tried to trivialize these deaths, but sometimes when the numbers were in the low hundreds, it sounded like, "and only 125 soldiers were killed this week." The tragedy really hit home when the June 27, 1969 edition of Life magazine published the faces of 242 people that were killed from May 28th through June 3rd. This was a random week picked by the magazine that had no particular significance, except for the families of those lost.

CHAPTER THIRTY

THE UNOFFICIAL STAGE OF KNIGHTHOOD

Yes, I was lucky that The Mechanic had remained my close friend as we entered high school. That is, until the day he tried to kill me. If he had been successful, the jury may have gone with the less culpable involuntary manslaughter defense. The Mechanic certainly did not have *malice aforethought*, as there was no willful intent to kill me, at least not on this occasion.

We had planned to hang out, as was our usual routine on weekend nights. We had heard rumor of a pink ribbon gathering and thought it would be a good idea to stop by and show our faces to score some points with the lovely ladies. The Mechanic also thought it would be fun to bring a guest. The guest's name was Jack, whom I had never met before. Jack's last name was Daniel's. The reason for an apostrophe at the end of the name is to show ownership. Jack owned Tennessee Whiskey No. 7. Jack would soon own our soul. Jack hung out with a hard-core gang that went by the name of "Liquid Courage". The Mechanic believed it would be in our best interest to acquire some of this liquid courage for ourselves prior to our visit to the pink side. He was sadly mistaken, and I would shortly join in on this error.

The Mechanic lived on the suicidal side of masochism as he "acquired" this 90 proof liquid from his dad's personal collection. I liked The Mechanic's dad, as he was a nice man like all the other C.I.A. dads in the Bowl. The Mechanic's dad was a former United States Marine. Marines are never ex-Marines. They will tell you they never stop being Marines. It's like an addiction; you live with it for the rest of your life. It is also as scary. I knew in my heart that behind this dad's smile was a horrific, indescribably brutal body count. There would be two more kills added to his total if the Marine dad had gotten wind of this theft.

The Mechanic was careful not to spill any of the contents from the uniquely square bottle. The glass vessel had a distinct black label affixed to it, one that evoked images of pirates and death. This was very appropriate. He smuggled the contraband out of the house in a clear mason jar, careful to not remove an amount that would be conspicuously missed. He should have poured it into a lead-lined container to shield us from the radioactivity. 90 Proof means it contained 45% alcohol. This means nothing because this mixture that had been carefully mellowed in fine oak barrels may well have been Kryptonite when poured into a thirteen-year old boy. When the manufacturer says the whiskey was mellowed, what they are really saying, is this is where the beautiful golden colored liquid develops its mean-spiritedness and mule kick. It was deceiving yet inviting at the same time.

We knew in our hearts that this was bad for us but we had been Knights of the Forest. We had fended off an invasion by the barbarian horde and done battle with would-be conquerors. Ok, so the barbarians were only First-Rounders, but they qualified by definition because they were rude, and no one really knows how many people are required to constitute an actual horde, but we did fight, and overcome, Mother Nature herself. Surely we could ingest several ounces of this hooch.

We managed to sip the God-awful stuff along the way to the pink ribbon gathering. With each step we became stronger and smarter and funnier, and I believe even a smidge taller. This magic elixir was lifechanging. How come no one had told us about this shit before? We forced it down until after a bit, we could barely tell that this stuff tasted like gasoline. It wasn't long before the Mason jar was empty, just in time to reach our destination. We were exuding coolness. The pink ribbons wouldn't be able to control themselves.

Apparently, the pink ribbons were totally in control and not vulnerable to our new super powers. Neither the Mechanic nor I would be able to provide any details of our visit, as particulars became quite fuzzy as the night progressed. We managed to depart the social event sooner than we had planned, after rapidly depleting all of our coolness. I do not recall the reason for the Hulk-like change that came over the Mechanic on our stagger home. For some reason, he wanted to fight me. We had never had so much as a disagreement since Kindergarten and now he wanted a piece of me.

I saw no reason not to fight him so we squared off on a stranger's front lawn. This was gong to be a better fight than when Gun took out the Black Hole. It was too bad we had no crowd to cheer us on. We circled each other intently under the moonlit sky. We were sizing up each other's stance and footwork. We were each planning the next move, when to move in for the killer shot. The Mechanic shuffled to his right. I was ready to strike the first blow when to my surprise, the Mechanic went down, hard. He had run into a low hanging tree

limb, striking his head and almost knocked himself out.
I guess I had won.

I lay down next to him on the grass contemplating our situation. We didn't have to wait long before Jack summoned his nasty stepbrother, Ralph O'Rourke. Ralph is one son-of-a-bitch. Ralph grabs your stomach and violently pulls it out of your body, spilling all the contents over whatever may be in the vicinity. Ralph, because he is a S.O.B., makes you call his name loud and clear, until your stomach is empty, and then some. This was the payment for the theft from a former Marine.

The Mechanic and I determined that our night out had come to an end after defiling the nicely manicured lawn of some unknown neighbor. We were lucky enough to experience projectile vomiting so we didn't have any mess on our clothes to explain to inquisitive parents. We managed to get ourselves home without any further incidents. The next day the Mechanic and I experienced flu-like symptoms that kept us in bed for a good part of the day. I'm guessing the moms knew better but figured we had suffered enough. We had gone through the unofficial stage of Knighthood, also referred to as Hell Knight. I did not meet up again with Jack for several decades after that night.

CHAPTER THIRTY-ONE

THE KNIGHT'S OATH FULFILLED

The woods are lovely, dark and deep,
But I have promises to keep,

- Robert Frost

My wife asked me where I was going and I told her I had some old business to take care of and would be awhile. I eased myself into my car and started the journey that I had promised many years ago. The hour drive went by quickly as memories flowed through my mind. As I pulled into the old neighborhood, I noticed that things looked a lot smaller except for the shade trees that lined the street. They were fully matured and almost obscured the homes they stood in front of.

I parked at the end of the houses where I remembered the entry path was to my Forest. It was barely visible and showed little use compared to the bare dirt path we had exposed after many trips in and out of our kid world. I immediately noticed that there was a drastic change in the landscape. Many of the trees were down or leaning precariously due to at least a couple of hurricane force storms. The weeds were severely overgrown and much of the ground was swamp like. Extensive building and development upstream prevented the rain from being absorbed back into the ground, which created more run-off that found its way to this forgotten uninhabited area that no one cared about any longer.

It was like I was standing in a different forest than the one I grew up in. It took me a few minutes to get my bearings and find my way to a familiar landmark but I managed to locate the Master. It was surrounded by a couple feet of murky water and looked at if it had a one-on-one battle with Mother Nature herself. Lightning strikes had amputated some larger limbs that hung, barely attached, at the tree's side, as if the Master had finally surrendered to her. There were no leaves on the lifeless giant as the forest insects and small rodents worked on the remains to return it to the forest floor.

I paused for a moment reflecting back on the Master's greatness. I imagine it was over 200 years old and hoped it had enjoyed its reign over the Forest and the time we spent with it. I then made my way through the almost impenetrable woods to my next destination. The sun was fading and sometimes light plays tricks on me so, I was unsure of what I was seeing as I approached Gray Rock. It looked like there was someone no, some people standing next to it.

As I emerged from the high grass, the figures turned in my direction and I could make out familiar features on their aged faces. Knapsack, Hoops, Rhino, and Skip were all standing there smiling at me. Before I could say a word, I felt something on my shoulder. At first I thought it was a branch and the Tree Man had returned for us but to my relief I found the Mechanic at the end of the outstretched arm.

I knew Bo wouldn't be joining us. I had heard that he committed suicide after a long struggle with drugs. I was twenty years old the last time I had seen Bo. I had been visiting my folks' house in between college semesters. I was driving through the old neighborhood and saw Bo walking down the street near his house. I hadn't kept in touch with him and thought it would be great to catch up. To my amazement, Bo was a completely different person. He had a faraway look in his eyes and was almost incoherent. It was impossible to hold a conversation with him so I politely excused myself and drove on.

That was the last time I ever saw Bo. I knew he had gotten into the drug scene shortly after we entered high school, but I had never imagined he had gone so far. Bo had survived the attack of the wasp swarm, the hangman's noose, and the death grip of the river, but he couldn't defeat his own demon. He shot himself not long after our brief encounter. I often regret not taking a few extra minutes with him that last day together. I know I couldn't have changed his life, but maybe...

I asked about the Gun. Skip looked down and said, "He didn't make it. Tommy didn't return from Vietnam." The unofficial war, which started before the Knights were born, raged on, and finally expanded into an evil behemoth, for the entire time we spent in the Forest. The war had silently paralleled our lives until it exploded in our faces during our high school years. It divided the entire country between the young hippies and the old establishment. The war finally caught up with the Gun soon after we graduated. When we turned eighteen in 1972, the military draft system was working overtime. I had a reasonably low number and waited it out but my number was never called. Tommy wasn't going to wait on a drawing to decide his future and went off and joined the Marines because that's the type of guy he was. I had heard rumors about him leaving but had no official word from anyone. President Nixon ended the war three short years later but not soon enough for Tommy.

Vietnam, the little unknown country that no one even knew where it was, claimed him from us as one of its victims. The horribleness that is war reached across a great ocean and then across an entire continent to grab a hold of one of our friends. KIA is the term used for military personnel "Killed In Action". They added Tommy's name to the list of 58,219 others.

Knapsack interrupted my thoughts when he said, "Its 7:17pm." It was July 7th, 2017 at 1717 hours. Six of the original Knights had returned to fulfill their vow that they had made 50 years earlier. It seemed heartless, but we were all thinking that six out of eight was pretty good, seeing how reckless we had been at an early age. We approached Gray Rock and all got down on our right knee the best that we could. We placed our right hands on the rock and repeated the word that we had said a half a century ago, "Knights of the Forest." I added, "And God Bless the lost Knights."

Skip noticed that there was a substantial crack in Gray Rock, caused by some unforeseen force of nature. There was a pile of gravel that had been created from this disturbance. It was as if these were seeds from the rock to be spread about the Forest to give new life and create other great rocks in another location. He grabbed a handful and gave each of us one as a memento to keep with us. I placed mine in my pocket.

We helped each other up from the damp ground and engaged in small talk catching up about our current activities and reciting the names of our grandchildren. We then made the obligatory promises to keep in touch and made halfhearted plans to meet again soon. We had kept our original promise to return to Gray Rock. As we exited our once great Forest to the street, we knew our childhood home was gone and the Knights were officially disbanded. We knew in our hearts we would probably never see each other again because life gets in the way.

I arrived home as darkness fell and my wife greeted me as I came through the door. She said, "Where have you been and why are your pants muddy"? I looked at her as I managed a half smile and said, "I was fulfilling my oath. Have a seat and let me tell you a story."

And miles to go before I sleep,

Vietnam's modern day struggle began as early as 1858 with France. The Vietnamese resisted being a colony through two world wars. After World War II, the spread of communism from the Soviet Union and China brought the United States into the fray and the identities and roles of combatants changed. At first Vietnam and the U.S. were allies but like many counties we had entered into an agreement with, the friendship turned to shit and we became mortal enemies. At the height of the undeclared war, there were over 500,000 U.S. troops deployed to Vietnam in 1968. This was a country slightly smaller than California. The last American solider left the country on March 29, 1973. The 58,220 casualties only accounted for the American military. In total, over three million people died in Vietnam and surrounding countries.

EPILOGUE

The following October, The Mechanic emailed me a an obituary that read as follows:

Benjamin 'Bud" Peterson 94

WWII Navy Veteran

Jupiter, Fl., formerly of Hillside, N.J., passed away on Friday, Oct 13, 2017. The funeral will be Tuesday, Oct. 17th at 9 a.m. from Queens Funeral Home, 1050 Liberty Ave., Hillside, NJ. The funeral mass will be celebrated at Christ The King Church in Hillside at 10 a.m. The interment will follow at Glendale Cemetery in Bloomfield, NJ. Visitors will be received at the funeral home on Monday from 3 to 7 pm.

Benjamin was a World War II Navy veteran and earned 10 Battle Stars while serving in the Pacific on the Attack Cargo Artillery ship, the U.S.S. Tyrell. Lt. Peterson assisted in delivering troops to the invasion of Okinawa Beach. He retired from St. Elizabeth's Hospital in Elizabeth, where he served as head pharmacist. Benjamin was predeceased by his wife, Mary, (Zimmerman), of 18 years. Donations can be made to the American Cancer Society in lieu of flowers.

It took me a few weeks before I was able to make it to the cemetery to pay my respects. I stopped at the office to obtain the exact location and then proceeded on to my destination. It was an old cemetery with very large headstones. The place looked more like a park than a cemetery, with large shade trees throughout the area. The cemetery appeared full but they continued to bury people every day. Many plots had been purchased decades ago for entire families, when people didn't move about the country with present day frequency. A few generations were interred in one location. I drove the empty winding road until I came to the landmark provided by the office employee. I parked my car and walked over a slight hill until I saw a patch of recently disturbed earth. The burial had not been long ago so the outline on the grave was still distinct and the earth was a rich brown color. The monument had already been in place before Bud had passed. All they had to do was engrave the latest information into the face of it. It read the same as his obituary with his name, birth, and death dates. Below that it said, Beloved Husband. His wife's name had been inscribed many years prior to Bud joining her for eternity. She had died in 1966, just a year before he saved all of us from the river. We never had a clue that she had been ill or that he spent the last year of her life taking care of her. He was a very private person and never let on to the agony he was going through. It wasn't until I walked closer to the grave that I saw it. It kind of blended into the surroundings, purposely camouflaged. It was an old, worn out, stained and tattered backpack. It was the same one that Knapsack had carried for so many years until Bo playfully stole it that fate full day, and almost died in the process, along with the rest of us. The Bud was a stranger to us when we were kids, who we feared, because we never got to know him prior to our rescue. We had pledged to watch over the Forest but The Bud had watched over us. It turned out that Bud was the true Knight of the Forest. Before I said goodbye to The Bud for the last time, I reached into my jacket pocket and removed a small gray rock. I carefully placed it on top of the headstone, beside the seven other matching stones, that had been placed there before I had arrived.

And miles to go before I sleep

GLOSSARY

ATOMIC BOMB — A VERY BAD THING THE UNITED STATES DROPPED ON JAPAN TO END WWII

BABY BOOMER — ANYONE BORN BETWEEN 1946 AND 1964 UNLESS THEY WERE BORN IN CANADA. THESE DATES CAN VARY ACCORDING TO WHO WANTS TO KNOW

BOOMER — LAST NAME ESIASON. RETIRED NFL QUARTERBACK PRESENTLY A COLOR COMMENTATOR FOR THE NETWORK

BUMMY — WHATEVER YOU WANT IT TO MEAN

CDC — HUGE GOVERNMENT AGENCY THAT NO ONE EVER WANTS TO HAVE SHOW UP AT THEIR HOME OR BUSINESS, SIMILAR TO IRS & FBI

CIA — ANOTHER ALPHABET ORGANIZATION WHERE ALL DADS WORKED

CIRCLE THE WAGONS — DEFENSIVE POSITION FOR A WAGON TRAIN, FROM THE OLD WEST TO TAKE, TO FEND OFF AN ATTACK OR THE 14TH ALBUM BY THE NORWEGIAN BAND DARKTHRONE

COLD WAR — THIS HAS NOTHING TO DO WITH TEMPERATURE OR WAR. IT WAS THE SUPER SPY ERA AFTER WWII THAT LASTED FROM 1947 TO 1991 WHEN RONALD REAGAN SAID OK THAT'S ENOUGH OF THAT AND THE SOVIET UNION SAID OK AND WENT HOME

COPERNICUS — FIRST FAMOUS SCIENTIST THAT WENT BY ONE NAME, THAT LATER INFLUENCED CHER & MADONNA'S CAREERS. HE WAS EXPELLED FROM SCHOOL FOR HIS INAPPROPRIATE MODEL OF THE SOLAR SYSTEM HE BROUGHT TO THE SCIENCE FAIR. FEBRUARY 19, 1473 TO MAY 24, 1543

DARWIN, CHARLES – SON OF ADAM & EVE, STATED THAT DUMB ASSES WON'T SURVIVE. HE WAS WRONG, THEY ARE STILL OUT THERE. FEBRUARY 12, 1809 TO APRIL 19, 1882

DOHICKYS - WHAT-CHA-MA-CALL-ITS, DOODADS, THINGAMAJIGS

DOODADS - THINGAMAJIGS, DOHICKYS, WHAT-CHA-MA-CALL-ITS

8MM FILM – ONE OF THE WORST NICHOLAS CAGE MOVIES IF YOU CAN REALLY SORT THEM OUT

ELVIS PRESLEY – IF YOU DON'T KNOW WHO HE IS YOU ARE BEYOND HOPE. JANUARY 8, 1935 TO AUGUST 16, 1977

FIDEL CASTRO – THE LITTLE GUERILLA THAT WOULD NOT DIE. ROOT CAUSE OF PRESIDENT KENNEDY'S LOWER BACK PAIN AUGUST 13, 1926 TO FINALLY NOVEMBER 25, 2016

FIRST ROUNDER – THE EVIL BABYBOOMERS

FOR PETE'S SAKE – STILL NO IDEA WHO PETE IS

GREATEST GENERATION – TOM BROKAW MADE A TRUCKLOAD OF MONEY COINING THIS PHRASE, WHICH HE TURNED INTO A BOOK OF THE SAME NAME. THIS WAS THE GROUP OF PEOPLE WHO LIVED THROUGH THE DEPRESSION AND WENT ON TO WIN WWII. THEY THEN CAME HOME AND CREATED THE BABY BOOM.

HITLER – WORST PERSON EVER, STARTED WWII THAT LED TO THE DEATHS OF OVER 50 MILLION PEOPLE WORLDWIDE

HOMEOWNER – THIS IS A MISNOMER BECAUSE USUALLY THE BANK OWNS THE HOME AND ALLOWS SOMEONE ELSE TO LIVE IN IT WHILE THE RENTER PAYS AN EXORBITANT AMOUNT OF MONEY TO THE BANK

JOE DIMAGGIO – MR. COFFEE. BASEBALL PLAYER ALSO KNOWN AS THE YANKEE CLIPPER, MOST FAMOUS SCORE WAS MARILYN MONROE

JOHNNY CASH – AMERICAN SINGER-SONGWRITER. ALSO CALLED SUE. FEBRUARY 26, 1932 TO SEPTEMBER 12, 2003

LSD – LUCY IN THE SKY WITH DIAMONDS WRITTEN BY THE BEATLES APPEARED ON THE SGT. PEPPER'S LONELY HEARTS CLUB BAND ALBUM

McCARTHY – THE CRAZY FIFTH BEATLE WHO FOUGHT COMMUNISTS

MARILYN MONROE – MALES DESIRED HER WHILE FEMALES WANTED TO BE HER. APPARENTLY LIVED AS A CANDLE IN THE WIND. JUNE 1, 1926 TO AUGUST 5, 1962

MERCURY ASTRONAUTS – THE COOLEST GUYS EVER EXCEPT THEY DIDN'T INCLUDE CHUCK YEAGER

MOBY DICK – LARGEST FISH EVER TO MAKE IT IN THE MOVIES EXCEPT HE WAS NOT A FISH

MOSES – THE MOST IMPORTANT PROPHET IN JUDAISM WHO FAILED TO RECOGNIZE THE PROFIT TO BE MADE WITH CHRISTMAS

NJ – PROPER NAME IS NEW JERSEY, ALSO CALLED JERSEY. IT REALLY SHOULD HAVE BEEN NAMED ANOTHER JERSEY, AS THE ORIGINAL JERSEY IS A BRITISH ISLAND IN THE ENGLISH CHANNEL

PARKWAY – A LANDSCAPED HIGHWAY THAT YOU USUALLY WIND UP PARKING UPON DUE TO INSUFFERABLE TRAFFIC

RAMBLER – A REAL AMERICAN CAR

ROBERT FROST – AMERICAN POET THAT HAD THE KNIGHTS OF THE FOREST IN MIND WHILE COMPOSING HIS FAMOUS WORKS MARCH 26, 1874 – JANUARY 29, 1963

ROSA PARKS – CIVIL RIGHTS ICON. SUCCEEDED IN POINTING OUT THE STUPIDITY OF SEGREGATION FEBRUARY 4, 1913 TO OCTOBER 24, 2005

SECOND ROUNDER – THE BEST BABY BOOMERS

SUBURBANITES – FORMER CITY DWELLERS THAT MOVED AWAY FROM THE CITY SO THEY COULD COMMUTE TO THE CITY EVERY DAY AND GO BACK THERE FOR ALL THEIR NEEDS AND ENTERTAINMENT

THERMONUCLEAR WAR — THE LAST PARTY REQUIRING SUN BLOCK 5000

THINGAMAJIGS - DOHICKYS, WHAT-CHA-MA-CALL-ITS, DOODADS

TOLL ROAD — LEGALIZED HIGHWAY ROBBERY, THE GIFT THAT NEVER STOPS GIVING

TOXIC WASTE — SEE NEW JERSEY

WHAT-CHA-MA-CALL-ITS - DOODADS, THINGAMAJIGS, DOHICKYS

ACKNOWLEDGEMENTS

Although this is a work of fiction, the story was based upon my life growing up in the real bowl. I would like to thank all the families of the bowl for looking out for all us kids and keeping us on the right path. All the parents shared the duties of correcting, scolding and praising all children, no matter what family.

I, would, like, to, thank, my, friend, Lori, Toth, for, removing, approximately, 900, unnecessary, comas, from, this, story, that, would, have, added, at, least, another, hour, to, the, read, time, and, prevent, me, from, sounding, like, Captain, Kirk. I, had, to, add, the, leftover, comas, here, as, I, didn't, know, what, else, to, do, with, them.

Much gratitude is also extended to my favorite artist, Bill Sly. He read my mind as to what exactly I wanted for this book and delivered without hesitation. Bill also designed the cover for my second book, *Just Plain Stupid*. Bill is an illustrator and designer with a long career in advertising and marketing. He studied fine art and commercial art at the deCret School of the Arts. He also studied oil painting under Harvey Dinnerstein at the National Academy in New York. I am also happy to call him a long time friend.

I would like to thank Cindy, my wife of numerous decades, for putting up with my post Knighthood quirks and craziness.

And my greatest appreciation goes to my sweet granddaughters, Nora and Dona, now entering their terrible twos. These beautiful girls have shown me that the second 60s could be even better than the first. They are truly my target audience. All my love to you, Gpa.

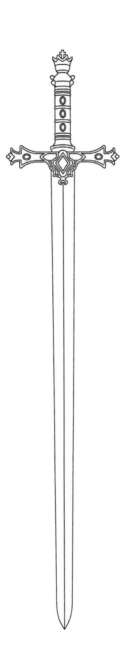